THE SECRET OF POPPYRIDGE COVE

SEASIDE INN MYSTERY
BOOK ONE

RIMMY LONDON

Copyright © 2022 by Rimmy London

All rights reserved.

No part of this book may be reproduced in any form or by any electronic or mechanical means, including information storage and retrieval systems, without written permission from the author, except for the use of brief quotations in a book review.

This is a work of fiction. Any similarities to persons living or dead is completely coincidental.

❀ Created with Vellum

For my dearest love

INTRODUCTION

Hello from Rimmy!

Bringing you one thrilling, fun, sweet, laugh-out-loud book at a time. I've so enjoyed these cozy mysteries and have plans for many more! I'd love to keep in touch. Here are a couple ways how…

*Follow me on Bookbub
(you'll get a notice when I have a new book out!)
*Subscribe to my newsletter
(Get a FREE BOOK just for signing up, and monthly mail from me!)

Cheers,
Rim

Seaside Inn Cozy Mystery series...
Book 1: The Secret of Poppyridge Cove
Book 2: A Traitor at Poppyridge Cove
Book 3: Stranded at Poppyridge Cove
Book 4: Danger at Poppyridge Cove

INTRODUCTION

Book 5: Murder at Poppyridge Cove
Book 6: A Poppyridge Cove Tragedy
Book 7: Lies at Poppyridge Cove

Megan Henny Cozy Mystery series...
Book 1: Two Shakes of a Hangman's Noose
Book 1: A Doggone Waterfront Shame
Book 2: Sniffing Out The Spy
Book 3: A Tail for Trouble (coming soon)

CHAPTER 1

The forest was ageless. Dark and rich with color, like the deepest part of Crystal Lake where Abby could remember swimming as a child. Redwoods were crowded with ferns and small pines among their massive trunks.

She breathed in the heavy pine smell, sweetened with the fragrance of sap that leaked from nearly every notch in the bark of a hundred trees. Her boyfriend, Chase, had yet to crest a small hill in the trail, and she waited for him in a giant shadow of the widest trunk she'd ever seen. It could span the width of her apartment, she was sure. It left her feeling powerful to be near it, and she wondered how she'd managed to live her life in the same state and never visit the redwoods.

Perched against the misty Northern California coastline, the woods had been invaded at every edge by tendrils of fog-like feelers, stretching out through the clearings in the trees. It was like a mysterious friend, haunting and welcoming together.

"Bee, where'd you go?"

Chase's voice called her back to the present, and she spun around with her deep brown curls bouncing. They naturally tightened in the coastal air, and she brushed a few tendrils out of her view.

"I'm here," she answered, just as she caught the first glimpse of him. The summer sun had tinted his honey-brown hair quickly this year, leaving lightened streaks of blonde threaded throughout. It was something she hadn't yet told him she admired. A smile crept across her face at the thought.

Emily and Ryan were farther down the trail, mutual friends they'd attempted to set up, but their bickering could be heard through the forest. The blind date wasn't going so well.

"I don't think they'll be thanking us," Chase whispered, glancing behind him as Emily's voice rang out.

"Why don't you just jump in your little yacht then and sail the seven seas? I'm sure that would be a great solution to world peace—at least for me."

Abby cringed, remembering her words again as she'd insisted Emily give Ryan a chance. "What are they even talking about?" she groaned, "Why do they have to debate the mysteries of the universe on their first date?"

Chase stood next to her and settled one hand against the bark of the mighty redwood. "I guess I should have told you Ryan isn't exactly chivalrous." He shrugged. "If he has something to say, he says it regardless of who he might offend."

Abby sighed and stepped under Chase's arm, happy at the way he easily dropped it around her, letting it settle heavy and comforting. Like a dance they'd rehearsed, their movements complimented each other naturally. It was something that came with time spent together, and they'd had a lot of that.

Emily trudged into view, her pixie-cut blonde hair pasted to her forehead in all the dewy mist. Her usual dedication to that selfie-ready appearance had vanished. She grumbled and scowled and finally lifted her eyes to Abby's.

Abby forced her mouth into a smile.

"I'm gonna take a minute," Emily growled, her eyebrows pressing even closer together as Ryan clomped up the trail behind her. She didn't acknowledge him and instead turned into the trees and continued until she was out of their view.

"Don't go too far, Em!" Abby yelled, knowing from experience not to press her friend. If she said she needed time, she meant it.

"Why can't you just be agreeable for one date?" Chase complained.

Ryan settled his hands on his hips and cast an irritated gaze to where Emily had last been seen stomping through the forest. "Well maybe if you'd set me up with someone who didn't constantly contradict me, I could!" He glanced at Abby. "Is she always like that? Seriously, every word out of my mouth seemed to be so repulsive she fought it off like an attack. And yeah, maybe I could have tried harder, but so could she!"

Abby shrugged, lifting her hands from her sides and searching for the words. She knew Emily could be a tough personality, but she was also fun and bubbly… when she wasn't picking a fight.

"Sorry Ryan," Abby finally said. "I'll go talk to her." She

slid her hand across Chase's strong back appreciatively, catching his eye in a parting glance before heading into the woods.

The ferns underfoot grew as she continued away from the trail, dampening her legs and boots. "Emily?" she called, stopping to listen for a reply.

There was a fluttering sound of birds leaving their roost at her intrusion as their wings beat against the branches above. "Can we talk, please?" She continued, walking in a wide arc around a particularly enthusiastic section of undergrowth. The small trail underfoot wasn't a trail at all—just a space between the ferns and trees that allowed her to move forward without the constant bath of fog-soaked underbrush.

The darkness deepened, and she looked up at the few patches of sky left. Trees almost completely blocked it out, and for the first time, she felt a twinge of fear at the absolute quiet around her. "Emily!" she called, harsh and almost angry. Why wouldn't she answer? She held on to a young tree and stepped around it, trying to squeeze through the brush.

Her foot skidded on a sudden drop-off, and she gasped, clinging to the tree. Hidden in ferns, a cliff dipped hundreds of feet down. It looked like a landslide that had scooped out the dirt and been overgrown again, leaving it completely camouflaged. Trees still grew right up to the edge, with a few angled outward, daring to steal the sunlight at a precarious angle. The ocean could be seen far beyond, cold and churning against the rocks and shoreline.

Abby panicked and searched with wide eyes. "Emily!" she shouted louder, and this time it was pitched with fear.

She swung around the way she'd come. "Chase!" Her voice echoed against the cliff and the trees, bouncing back to her. "Ryan!"

Someone.

"Are you okay?" Chase's voice came from all around, first one direction and then another. "Where are you?"

Abby spun around, searching out his voice. She'd been sure of her route, but now it all looked completely foreign. She turned again, scanning the trees to her right. And then her left. "I can't find her!" she shouted, hearing movement in the brush from far off.

"Just come this way," Chase shouted again, and Abby turned to her left, stepping over ferns and berry bushes and weaving between trees.

"We're coming," Ryan yelled.

"Follow my voice," Chase repeated, but this time, the sound seemed to come from behind her, by the cliff. She turned, confused. Had they already passed her? She started to backtrack the way she'd come. A small trail appeared between the ferns and led around the cliff, farther down the coastline. Perhaps Emily had found it too. She followed it slowly, cautious of how much ground she'd traveled.

"Emily?" she called again. There were faint impressions of footprints in the trail, and her mind reeled. What if Emily *couldn't* answer? What if she'd been running down the trail—how much farther would she have gone by now? What if she fell? Abby took off at a run, jumping over roots and rocks and letting the decline move her legs faster.

It wasn't until her arm brushed against the worn wood that she noticed the rickety, faded fence along one side.

She slowed to a walk and rounded another tight grove of trees. But then she stopped in her tracks.

A mansion stood beyond the trail, spread out in what she could imagine used to be complete luxury. It was badly faded and nearly falling apart, with a railing that only had two rungs left. Various spots in the siding had broken away completely, leaving crumbled, splintered piles of wood framing its foundation.

But the view.

It stood on a cleared section of land, facing the Pacific coastline, with almost a 360 degree view of the glorious ocean. From her current vantage point, the cliff was considerably lower, and a wood-and-rope trail could be seen at the edge, as if the climb down to the beach were merely a stroll.

Abby's heart was beating hard. And while she still felt anxious for her friend, she'd become dizzy with excitement. The house was incredible and so obviously abandoned. Perched between the ocean and the deep redwoods like absolute perfection.

She'd never thought of owning her own home, let alone fixing something like this up. But to imagine gazing out at that coastline for every sunrise and sunset was like a dream she'd never fully developed. Only now it blazed in her mind and surged through her veins. She belonged here.

A breeze pushed past her, and she wrinkled her nose. Sewage and rot filled her nose, and she choked on her next breath. She covered her mouth with one hand, feeling suddenly sick. The breeze shifted just in time, bringing sweet, fresh ocean air. A hint of wild poppies cleared her head, and she pulled in a deep breath, stepping into the breeze and away from whatever had nearly gagged her.

"Abby!"

She could hear Chase calling, but the stillness of the house made her hesitate. It felt like she'd found something that could fleet away at the slightest disturbance. She walked past the structure, gazing out at the ocean and what now could be seen as more of a hill than a cliff. It was exquisite. Abby's eyes drank it in, scanning the view and every inch of untouched wilderness. The coastal breeze pushed her hair back and whipped at her shirt, then relented.

When it lifted again, she was surrounded full force. A smell like death itself, pushing its way down her throat and filling her lungs. Her eyes stung with it, and her skin crawled. She choked out a breath, forcing the smell from inside her and clamping both hands over her face.

Spinning around, she glimpsed the back porch for the first time. It was littered with the most repulsive sight she'd ever seen.

A tangled mess of fur and claws, wings and tails. Birds, raccoons, cats, and even a large yellow dog. Her heart broke, and then her eyes widened as she suddenly realized what was similar about every variety of dead animal. A shock jolted from her head to her toes. Each one had been decapitated, with its head lying on top of or next to its body. Dark stains of what she could only imagine used to be fresh blood were visible on almost the entirety of the deck, with one paw mark streaking down the side of the house.

Her head began to spin, the scene before her swaying nauseatingly until she wasn't sure what was real and what was imagining. A moment before, she'd been reeling from the euphoric vision of adventure the estate symbolized, and now she was reeling from something else.

She tore her gaze away and ran, her throat strangled and stomach churning, holding back a scream. Past the house and toward the trail, until suddenly she felt her stomach revolt. Lunging for the nearest tree trunk, she was overcome with sickness, leaning into the bushes. It didn't relent until her stomach was empty, and she was left coughing and gasping for breath.

"Abby!"

Chase sounded terrified, and Abby tried to find her voice. But he raced down the trail before she had the chance. She was sure her face was ashen white.

"What happened?" He held her shoulders, steadying her as she swayed on her knees. He glanced into the bushes. "Are you ill?"

Abby shook her head, bringing her hand to her forehead. It felt clammy and cool.

Dead.

She swallowed suddenly, forcing the images from her mind. "No," she said weakly, "I just saw something."

Chase kept a strong arm around her, supporting her. "Well, what on earth was it?" But he'd also caught sight of the house, and in between concerned glances for Abby, he gazed at it.

Emily and Ryan came down the trail, eyes wide as they took in Abby's face and then the house beyond.

Abby could tell by the faint ring of red around Emily's eyes that she'd been crying. And as proud as she knew her friend to be, she guessed that was why she hadn't answered their calls. After all, they'd known each other since the third grade, and Abby had never seen her cry. She studied the way Ryan navigated around her, like he was being careful to place himself where she might need him. Like he wanted to be close to her.

Emily had changed as well. She no longer glared at Ryan. Instead, her eyes found him again and again, as if she was curious. And perhaps interested.

Abby's shock began to clear, leaving warmth in her face and a settled calm in her mind. The group, turning to her expectantly, was poised and waiting. They observed the color returning to her cheeks in perplexed silence.

Finally, it was Chase who spoke. He looked deeply into Abby's eyes, resting a hand on her arm.

"What did you see?"

CHAPTER 2

The drive back to San Francisco was unusually quiet, with bits of polite conversation here and there. Abby couldn't help but marvel again at how the dynamics between Ryan and Emily had changed completely. Their conversation in the back seat was unremarkable, mostly focused on comments about the view as they passed. But in between was a heavy space of quiet, and Abby wondered if their eyes were doing more talking than their lips.

She fought the urge to glance back and watch them, curious to see if her hunch was right and Emily really was developing an interest in Chase. Or she'd been so deflated after crying that she'd given up the desire to argue. Abby hoped it was the first option.

"I still can't believe all those animals," Emily said.

Abby glanced back to see her sitting a little closer to Ryan than when they'd first entered the car. She smiled.

"It was definitely a shock," Abby agreed, "but really, we were so deep in the forest. I'd bet that place has been abandoned for a century. It's probably just become a dumping ground for wild animals."

Abby had come up with this idea as they'd walked out of the forest, and she wanted so badly to believe it. The house was still aching to belong to her, and though she hadn't confessed it to her friends, she was planning on finding out who owned it, if anyone. Her meager starting salary would never be enough, but she didn't care. She'd find a way.

Chase's eyebrows had risen in a wide arc, although he didn't speak right away. Abby hoped that meant he was going to let her idea stay awhile.

But he finally shook his head. His voice was serious where hers had been light. "I don't think so, Abby," he glanced across her face with his lips stretched into a grim line. "I've never seen a wild animal do *that*."

The pit of Abby's stomach sunk deep and heavy, and she looked back out the window with her eyes scanning the view. Instead of housing developments and coastal shops, her mind was bombarded with torn animal carcasses, heaped up and left to decay.

"Why would anyone kill a bunch of animals and leave them at an abandoned house?" Ryan's question hung heavy in the car. His shock and disbelief at what they'd seen were etched into each word, and it seemed no one knew how to answer. The car hung in silence until they eventually crossed the Bay Bridge.

Abby spied her favorite shop in all of San Francisco. "Let's stop and pick up some sourdough," she offered, looking back to see Ryan and Emily agreeing with her. Their hands were lying very close together on the seat, as if they'd suddenly released their hold.

Abby faced front again, catching a sly grin from Chase as she did. "That sounds like a great idea," he said, dropping their musings and giving her a wink. A smile spread out on her face as well, and she turned to the window, hiding it from the backseat.

* * *

THE SHOP WAS as delicious to look at as its sourdough was to eat. Tall windows, stacked one upon the other, let the light become a focal point. Night was just settling in, and the store seemed to glow beautifully in its dusky surroundings.

They gazed up at a giant, towering silo as they entered that left Abby feeling wondrously small.

She couldn't help stopping at the entrance when she spotted rows of magazines displayed against the wall near a drinking fountain. After a quick scan of their titles, she finally found what she'd been searching for: *Coastal Fixer-uppers For Sale: Northern California.*

She snatched it from the shelf and began flipping pages while following Chase to the display case. No one had noticed her distraction; they chatted pleasantly about artisan breads, rolls, and loaves.

And then she saw it. The same rickety, abandoned house. Even in its obvious neglect, it was beautiful. Windows larger than they should have been at the time it was built. A few were broken, but they were obviously placed to take advantage of the sprawling coastline views. The dimensions seemed more modern than she'd noticed, and it complimented the rugged wilderness surrounding it like a sparkling gem on the neck of a beautiful woman. To Abby, all it needed was a little shine.

Just imagine if it were new again.

She couldn't help but picture it. The house called to her. It seemed built just for her—the perfect balance of wilderness and escape, with enough luxury to satisfy even the pickiest customer… once it was refinished, of course. Abby's enthusiasm intensified as she pictured individual apartments and guests pulling up to the private, ocean's edge escape. Hundreds of lights and pine wreaths during the holiday season.

And then it all crumbled away when she spotted the price. A number two… with six zeros behind it.

"Two million dollars?" she blurted out.

"What's two million?" Emily asked. She stepped aside Abby and looked down at the magazine. "Oh," she glanced up at Abby curiously.

"Abby," Chase's voice chimed in, and although he hadn't yet looked at the picture in the magazine, he seemed to know what it was. "Why does it matter how much it costs?" He glanced down at the page and back at her face. "You weren't seriously…"

He paused, stopping his thought and studying her instead. "Who knows what's going on out there. Some of those animals were killed fairly recently. They hadn't been dead that long."

Abby still gazed at the page. "Well, what if it is just some wild animal? Wolves have been seen in the redwoods before."

Chase didn't look the least bit swayed, but he let it drop. "Well, even so, it would take twice what they're asking just to fix up an abandoned shell like that." His focus lifted from Abby to the man in line behind her. He was tall, able to see the page from where he stood, and obviously listening in on their conversation.

"Very sorry to intrude," the man said. He reached forward and tapped the picture. "But I thought you might be interested to know a bit about it. I'm a local realtor."

Abby didn't care what anyone else wanted. She couldn't believe her good fortune and nodded enthusiastically. To her, this was a very physical sign that her life was meant to be connected to this old mansion. Chills broke out on her arms.

The man smiled. "Well, this house has been on the market for decades on and off. They can't seem to find a buyer who will stick. But judging from your comments earlier, you've seen why." He looked at every member of his small audience before continuing. "Even the neighbors stay clear of the property. But in my opinion, it's the most picturesque home and prime location in all of California. Someone will buy it eventually, and they won't run away."

"There are neighbors?" Abby asked. She shifted her weight from one foot to the next, anxious for the answer.

The man nodded. "About half a mile down the coastline. Six or seven homes. I guess you could call them neighbors. They're either retired and living quite well or large rental homes that mostly sit vacant. It's a very prestigious area."

The line moved forward with Emily and Ryan turning from the conversation to study the breads together. Chase turned to the counter as well, but Abby whispered one more question.

"Is the price firm?" She imagined if it could somehow be lowered just a touch, her and Chase could possibly...

But the thought withered and died as quickly as it came. She hardly had a full-time income, and Chase, although his private therapy practice was very successful, had already made his disapproval known.

"It is. Very firm," the man answered. He was looking up at the displays of breads now, and Abby reluctantly turned to them as well. Chase was eyeing her but didn't comment again about the house. Instead, he handed her a long loaf of sourdough wrapped in brown paper.

She pulled a piece off the end. The crust crackled when she pinched it and a soft, fluffy interior released a tiny cloud of steam. "Mmm," she murmured, chewing the fresh-from-the-oven sourdough and forgetting about anything else for a moment.

Why was she pressing it, anyway? Two million was so far out of her budget it was laughable. And like Chase said, she would need at least double that to fix it up. She was worrying over nothing. Whatever dreams had burst from her out in the woods, they were only that. Dreams.

Still, she rolled up the magazine and tucked it under one arm, entertaining the thought of buying a lottery ticket on the way home.

After dropping off Emily and Ryan at their homes, where Ryan hugged Emily in parting, Chase parked in front of Abby's apartment. From the outside, it looked like a modestly sized townhome, sandwiched between other similar builds in different shades of color. But the reality was she only called the top half home.

Which meant it was tiny.

Chase's apartment, while only a couple blocks away, was considerably larger and surrounded by other professionals that boasted prestigious initials after their names. Initials like MD, DC, or DMD.

"Thanks for the ride," Abby said, brushing a kiss across his lips and reaching for the door. She was itching to read more about the house, even though she could see in Chase's eyes that he wanted to talk to her. She hesitated, waiting for him to say whatever was brewing in his mind.

"I understand how adventurous and opportune that house seems." He shook his head, smiling. "It's like a physical manifestation of your soul. I get that."

Abby loved the way he used words. But she could tell he wasn't finished and was hesitant to hear what else was going on in that handsome head of his.

"But in truth, Abby, I worry that this isn't something we could ever reasonably finish. There's always something new and shiny that looks better than what you have now... but it's just not. You can't live life always eager to drop what you have for something *better*."

And there it was. His assessment of her. He'd said *we*, but the truth was his therapist's side was digging deep into her problems and *propensities*. Abby felt an argument brewing in her chest, but she didn't release it. Not yet.

"I know I get distracted by ideas and new goals," she began. "Nearly every day I come up with something I could start or learn, or start *to* learn. It's a hard habit to kick, to try to force myself to just be content with my career. But really, I'm not. I'm not happy with my career—and it's not a career. It's a job!"

"It's a good job," Chase argued.

"Really?" Abby hadn't meant to raise her voice, but it

rose just the same. "Designing labels? You think I should be totally happy with that? Helping people select just the right peanut butter wasn't really what I had in mind when I chose design."

"So look for a new job, then," he said simply, hand lifted in the air like it was that easy.

Abby crossed her arms in front of her, releasing a gust of breath. "It's really nothing to argue about anyway," she grumped. "It's not like I have millions of dollars to spend."

Chase didn't answer and looked nervously back at her, like he wasn't sure how to continue.

But what she hadn't confessed was she'd already tried. She'd looked for a job—*had* been looking for a job. For months now, and there was nothing. Especially if she wanted to stay close to Chase, which she did, then it wasn't even worth taking the time to look. Design was almost the number one major chosen in the area, and who wouldn't want to start their design company in San Francisco?

But if she could remodel a place like that, it would be the perfect portfolio on display for everyone to see. A designer retreat. And sure, it was a silly dream, but it struck a nerve with her that Chase would argue about something she couldn't have, anyway. To not even be given the slightest hope of ever proving him wrong was infuriating.

She glanced over at him, and her anger softened at the turn of his lips. She could see the apology written clearly in his eyes before he said it.

"I'm sorry." He sighed. "I'm sorry I always rush to dampen that fire you have. I really do love you for it." He chuckled. "I don't know anyone else in the world who would see actual potential in that place."

Abby released all her pent-up anger in a single breath. "I know," she breathed. "It's so obviously a disaster. But honestly, I've never felt like this." She glanced at him as she continued cautiously sharing pieces of her heart. "I didn't even realize I could love a house so deeply—like it was meant to be mine. It's like I had no control over what I was feeling. If there was any way for me to buy it right this second, I would."

Chase studied her face, falling into a contemplative silence. Abby wasn't sure if he was feeling motivated by her little confession, or if he was questioning his association with someone so clearly out of their mind. Either way, she couldn't shake the thoughts that were still pulsing in her mind—in her heart. Somehow, she had to go see it again.

CHAPTER 3

The next morning, Abby ran the hills in her neighborhood, followed by a long, hot shower. The air in San Fran was always partially cold, even in the summer… and especially in the mornings. But she liked the chill, it was refreshing and brisk.

She found an envelope in her mailbox, alongside a handful of junk mail and a magazine selling festive nuts, and slid a knife along the top of the rather thick paper. It was penned by hand, in letters that curled. Not only was there a letter, but official-looking documents. Abby narrowed her eyes, settling at the small card table that was her breakfast nook. She rubbed her wet hair with a towel one more time and began reading.

Dearest niece,

You don't know me, but for a long time I've known you were the most like me of anyone in the family.

"Huh." Abby turned the letter over and read the name quickly. Sharalyn Ernest. She'd never heard the name

Sharalyn before, but she recognized Ernest as her mother's maiden name.

Let me first introduce myself. I am your great-aunt, whom you've never met. I've been keeping a close eye on you since you were born. There are times when an old lady knows something of destiny, and you and I share a connection. You were born on a night that raged with storm and wind to parents that battled almost as fiercely. And yet, you were delicate and bright—kind beyond your understanding and indeed beyond your experience.

Abby set the paper down with her eyes stinging. The memories of her parent's arguments lashed out at her, as if they'd happened that very day instead of years ago. It made her angry that this woman she'd never met would know such intimate things about her life, and in more detail than she'd ever shared with anyone, including those closest to her. Including Chase.

With a *hmph*, she kept reading.

I, too, was born into a family that was anything but loving. And yet, almost beyond my control, I have an intense love of life. A love of people. I see their contentment with the controlled cages they've built for themselves, and I wish they would understand what life is truly for. I wish they would know what it means to dream and achieve, for I have done both.

Abby's eyebrows rose, and she turned the page over to read the last few lines in disbelief.

You are to be the steward of my estate when I pass, at which time this letter will be sent. I apologize deeply for never having met you, but when my body became frail and weak, it wasn't the state I would have you remember. In this, I am too proud, but I'm sure you can understand a certain dignity in life. Just know that I will be watching you from heaven, anxious to see what magic you work with the resources you've now inherited.

—I love you, Bee

Abby gasped, dropping the page to the table as chills erupted like a rash on her skin. Her mind twisted and worked to put the pieces together, but it seemed impossible. Or perhaps an elaborate prank. Very elaborate. *Bee?* Only Chase had ever called her that. And if, indeed, this was some eccentric rich relative…

She shook her head. No. There was no way. Things like this didn't happen in real life. Besides, she was sure her mother would have mentioned a rich aunt, as much as she enjoyed draining the resources from everyone around her. Abby squeezed her eyes closed, pressing her hands to her face and stopping the anger before it could spread.

Straightening in her seat, she flipped through the few additional pages. There was a small 3x5 picture of a woman who looked to be in her sixties. She was very dignified and proud, but her wide smile showed generous kindness. It fit perfectly with the letter. Abby swallowed and lifted the next page. It was of a beautiful brick building. England, it looked like. The sign in front said SOLD.

The last page she stared at the longest, wondering just what type of sick person would go to such lengths for a trick. It was a bank statement, with a final balance well into nine figures. Abby swallowed, glancing at a name and phone number handwritten at the top, with directions to call and make arrangements. She swayed a little in her seat before finally remembering to breathe.

"It's not real," she mumbled, standing and leaving the papers spread out across the table. "*This* is real."

She forced herself to critique her living space. The half-sized fridge that looked like it had been beaten with a baseball bat by its previous owner. The dingy kitchen that remained soiled and stained no matter how hard she scrubbed. The faucet that leaked even after Chase had replaced it with a newer model. Linoleum floors that were cracked and peeling up at the edges. Walls splattered with some unknown grease spots that refused to come off. This was reality. *Her* reality.

It was with a spiteful resolve that she snatched up her cell phone and pushed the numbers. She'd let them have it. No one was going to weasel one cent out of her. The line rang only once, giving her hardly enough time to organize her thoughts when a mature voice answered.

"Good morning, Blakney Law Offices,"

"Oh," she glanced down at the paper. "I was trying to reach, um, Mr. Thomas Blakney?"

"And who's calling, Miss?"

"This is Abby Tanner." She kicked herself for using her last name and imagined someone eagerly scribbling her information down, perhaps chortling an evil laugh at the same time. As she waited, her jaw set into a firm tilt.

"Abigail!" The voice was enthralled, cheering her name through the line, like it was the reunion of a cherished friendship.

Abby fidgeted with the paper, reading it again and feeling utterly baffled. Were they this good? "Yes," she finally answered. "I received a letter today, and I need to speak with you about it. I don't appreciate—"

"My dear, I can't tell you how long I've been waiting to meet you," he continued with a hint of English accent that sounded very professional. "Your aunt spoke of you nearly ten years ago. I had a time trying to convince her to take the trip and see you, and sadly, in the end, she

refused. A proud woman, but more generous than even her family knew."

He paused, and Abby stood with her mouth open, unsure of what was going on.

"Now, I can only imagine the surprise that letter caused," the man continued, "and the questions you must have. I'd love to meet with you as soon as possible—"

"I know it's a hoax!" she shouted, hearing the *crazy* in her voice. She needed to cool it. After a steadying breath, she tried again. The other end of the line had gone silent, and she was glad. The man only confused her.

"I may be young, but don't think I'm so foolish to believe I've just inherited 200 million dollars." She laughed like a dry, shaky cord from a tone-deaf choir. "From some unknown, doting aunt. *Right*. I just called to tell you I'm going to report you and your law office. This is despicable and should be punished!"

She pressed end before the man could answer, her hands shaking and throat so dry she could hardly swallow. Her forehead was perspiring. She brushed it with one arm while still holding the papers in one hand and her cell phone in the other. It was crazy. Delusional. And it made her angry that they might attempt to fool others too. Maybe some poor, unsuspecting, innocent person who would fall for it without question.

She glared again at the papers and dialed the local police office.

CHAPTER 4

Chase had been thinking over their trip to the redwoods almost non-stop. To him, the house had been horrifying. A nightmare. Something he would visit on Halloween to frighten his little brother. Add in the mutilated animals, and it was grounds for a proper horror film.

But when he'd seen how completely lost Abigail had been in the idea of owning it, he'd genuinely tried seeing it from her angle. Her completely awestruck face. He'd known her for nearly five years, and he'd never seen her so passionate about anything before. Even her career was merely something she pursued because she naturally did well in design. It was second nature for her to piece things together beautifully.

So maybe I should trust her and the inner potential she sees in the place.

He grimaced. It was a hard thought to swallow.

Walking from his office to her apartment, he hoped to have a more encouraging conversation than the day before. Having been left with a couple of hours of free time—after his second patient of the morning canceled—he wanted to surprise her.

He rang the doorbell and listened to the melody of chimes inside. It made him laugh. Something like that would drive him crazy. Just a simple ding-dong would suffice. But it fit her. Always making things better and more beautiful than the standard.

When he was left standing longer than usual, he leaned to the side and peered through the adjacent window. The glass was warped, but he caught her blurred silhouette walking forward slowly. Very slowly.

Finally, the door opened, and she stood there with her phone still pressed to her ear. "You're absolutely sure about this? The company has been looked into?" Her eyes looked somewhat glazed, and her hair hung damp at her shoulders from a recent shower.

Chase inched forward, but Abby still stood square in the doorway and didn't seem to notice. Her mouth was hanging open a bit. Chase tried to listen to the deep voice on the other end of the line, but it was too quiet.

"So--" Abby stopped, listening. "No, I'm sorry. Yes, I believe you. I do. I'm just… yeah, a bit shocked. Okay, thank you so much for your help."

Her arm dropped to her side, and she finally acknowledged Chase. But it was just a blank stare, as if he were a hologram and something was interesting behind him.

"Is everything all right?" Chase asked cautiously, turning around to glance into the street before twisting back to her again. She hadn't moved. "Can I come in?"

"Oh, um…" Abby stepped back and held the door open for him. She was taking deep, silent breaths, and a strange look settled on her features. Chase couldn't pinpoint the expression.

"Hey." He touched her arms cautiously, not wanting to push her over whatever edge she was balanced on. He knew enough about human behavior to see she was overwhelmed. But his touch seemed to work. She flinched and came back to the present.

"Oh my gosh, Chase," she breathed. Her eyes became shiny, and she swallowed hard with her lip shaking.

"What is it?" he asked again, feeling panicked now. But a smile had shown on her face, big enough to display her incredible set of dimples. He loved those.

"I still can't believe it, but I've inherited…" She laughed suddenly, shaking her head. Her dark curls bounced around her. "Something."

"You've inherited something?" he asked, thoroughly confused. Her dad had been out of the picture since she was a teenager, and her mother died a few years prior—complications from her many addictions. As for her other relatives, they were less than involved in her life.

But she nodded, confirming it. "I didn't believe it, so I called the police. They checked in on the company and…" Her breath came out in a gust, and she swayed on her feet. But the dimples were still going strong. "Here," she said, handing him the paper in her hand.

He read it quickly, flipping it over to discover the sum.

Two hundred million dollars.

"You don't know who this is?" he asked, the question coming out in a whisper of shock. But his mind had already wrapped around the idea. People inherited large sums of money all the time—and then a year or two later they ended up in his office discussing the many repercussions of their bad decisions. He shook the thought off. This was Abigail he was talking about. She wouldn't do anything like that.

He glanced up at her. The grin remained, wide and gloriously beautiful. His heart warmed at the sight.

"I've never heard of her." She was speaking quickly. "I'm sure if my mother had known there were relatives left to swindle, she would have mentioned it. This aunt must have known as much and kept her fortune a secret. I don't know!"

"This is incredible," Chase's voice was quiet, and he'd begun to fight his natural tendency to analyze. He wanted to enjoy this moment and be happy for Abigail. "So what do you need to do? Did you call this number?" He pointed to the penciled-in note and watched Abigail's cheeks flush ever so slightly.

"Well, yeah. I did." She giggled. "I accused them of being a fraud."

Chase's lips finally stretched into a smile, and he laughed. He could easily imagine her conversation. She laughed with him and stepped into his arms, resting her head on his chest in the hug he loved best. The one where she surrendered, leaning against him like he was so very needed.

But in reality, if she had just inherited a fortune, did she need him anymore? Chase tried to brush the irritating thought away, but it stuck like a burr, tangled uncomfortably close to his skin.

"So, I guess I should call them back," Abigail said, leaving his embrace and pressing a button on her phone.

She pushed speaker and glanced up at Chase as they settled together on the couch.

The line connected and Chase notice a trembling in Abigail's hand as her phone shook slightly.

"Well, good morning again," the cheery gentleman said. "I thought you might be calling back."

"Sorry about that," Abigail bit her lip, smiling at the same time.

"Oh, no, no problem at all. We quite understand. You'd be amazed by the lengths we have to go to sometimes to get a client to believe us." Some papers shuffled in the background. "Now, we'd like to meet with you as soon as possible. When would be a convenient time for you to travel? A few days should be fine."

"I'm sorry?" Abigail asked, looking up at Chase again. He shrugged.

"We need to meet with you here in the office in London, ma'am. I apologize for not explaining that earlier—I thought you knew."

"Oh."

Chase could tell Abigail's head was swimming. He rubbed her back.

"Would this week be okay? If you're able to, I'd love to have you here on Thursday. Everything is paid for through your aunt's estate, so there's no concern there."

Now Chase's head was swimming. He stared back at Abigail, awaiting her response.

"Yes, I guess that would be fine," she finally answered. Her eyes jumped back to Chase. "Could I bring someone with me?"

"Of course, no problem at all. I'll send you some

papers to fill out, and we'll get these tickets arranged. Thank you so much, Ms. Tanner."

"You're welcome."

The line disconnected, and they sat quietly for a moment with Chase already mentally clearing his schedule. He'd have to take on double the patient load next week. But that was hardly anything to consider.

They were going to London.

Silence stretched on as they both battled to grasp the sudden change in their lives.

Abigail stood slowly, gazing out across her tiny apartment. "I don't believe this," she whispered, trance-like and dull.

"It's a lot to take in Abby," Chase said, standing next to her and studying her face. But when her dimples appeared again, deep and joyful, he couldn't help but grin with her. A cheek-aching, eye-reaching, all-teeth-showing grin.

Laughter broke through his skepticism, and she joined loudly, drowning him out and squealing when he wrapped her up and lifted her off the floor. He spun her around, amazed and overwhelmed and blissfully happy for this incredible woman, who'd never had more than a few dollars as a child. He loved her beyond words, and she'd just been granted every wish she'd never dared to hope for. Everything he'd ever wanted for her.

He set her down and held her, breathing hard. Her heart was beating wildly in her chest as she sighed, and laughed, and sighed again. Chase leaned away just enough to look into her widened eyes.

"Buy the house," he said.

Her face sobered, and her gaze searched their dingy

surroundings before returning to him. "Do you think I should?" she asked, her eyebrows pressing together in thought.

"I've never seen someone fall so instantly in love before," he said, winking. Her lips pressed together in a sly grin. "You should go for it."

Slowly, she clasped her hands with each of his, leaning against him and looking deeply into his eyes. He relished the warmth that spread through his chest and delightfully scattered his thoughts. "I'll only do it if you're with me," she answered. Clear, thought out. Sensible.

A rush of love for this woman filled him as she gazed up at him and waited. Like his opinion was worth everything to her. Like she needed him.

"I'm with you, Abigail," he whispered, releasing her hands to settle his own on her honey-cream face. He trailed his hands slowly along her delicate jawline, smiling as her eyes closed and the tension between her brows smoothed away. He closed the distance between them, watching her beautiful face until his own eyes closed and their lips met.

She was tonic to his soul, and he couldn't remember ever kissing her this way before. The cares of the world were no longer theirs. It left him with every sense and thought focused on this moment.

When she leaned away and placed her hand on his face, he leaned back too. It was like stopping himself midfall. Like fighting gravity. He smiled back at her with the dizzy feeling of being intoxicated but hoped it didn't show.

"When do you need to get back to the office?" she

asked. "I'm sorry if it'll be hard clearing your schedule, but…" A grin appeared on her face again.

"It's no problem," he assured. He glanced at the small circular clock above the stove, hardly able to believe it'd been over an hour. "I do need to get back though."

"Okay." She looked down at her phone again. "Come over later and we'll get these papers filled out."

"London," he said.

Her eyes lit up. "London."

CHAPTER 5

Hardly one week later and the first-class flight had been more luxury than Abby had experienced before, with seats wide and soft enough to fall comfortably to sleep. And the food! Rich and delicious, served with gleaming silverware and fresh-squeezed orange juice.

Stepping out of the airport and into the busy heart of London, however, was vaguely like a Harry Potter movie. Accents, fog, and trendy scarves abounded. The history of the city was revealed in the many lavish stone and brick buildings, aged but still so much more beautiful than their hastily erected, modern neighbors.

She'd given Chase the task of a navigator, and he took to it like the naturally centered being he was. In one hand, he held his phone with the image of a map on the screen, and in the other, the handle to his luggage.

"Let's head this direction." He tilted his head down the sidewalk to their right. "If you don't mind towing your luggage for a bit."

Abby agreed wholeheartedly, excited to tread the streets of London. The thrill of being in a new country filled her with unlimited energy, even though she should have been exhausted from traveling. She was nearly giddy.

"I can't believe we're here," she huffed, walking as quickly as she could. She trailed behind Chase briefly to let passing pedestrians by, then skipped up to a jog until they were side-by-side again. "And two days ago, we had no idea our lives would change course. Just like that. *Bang.* And now we're in London!"

Chase looked up from his phone and laughed lightly. "I guess I hadn't thought of it like that." He shrugged. "But you're right. It's pretty amazing." He looked back at his phone and slowed. "Should be right here."

They stood at the base of one of those aged buildings Abby had admired. It was tall and made of white stone, flecked with sandy brown throughout. The gargoyles and curled edges were mesmerizing.

"Wow," Abby murmured. Her heart had begun to thump in her chest as she wondered just what this meeting would entail. It was an incredible fortune, and she couldn't imagine them just handing her a paper to sign. Would she need to prove her identity? Would they ask her personal questions?

Her smile wavered.

"Bee?" Chase stood holding the door open, waiting, and Abby shook herself from her thoughts.

Everything will be fine. Don't panic.

And yet, even with her self-warning, Abby couldn't help but continue the speculations as they read the gold-etched sign on the wall and rode the elevator up to the twentieth floor. What if there had been some terrible mistake, and she wasn't the right person? What then? She'd never seen this aunt or even heard of her. Maybe Sharalyn had contacted the wrong girl. Maybe they weren't even related!

"It'll be fine," Chase said in the quiet of the elevator.

Abby's eyes flicked up to meet his. They felt a little dry, as if they'd been open too wide for too long. She blinked, but couldn't get herself to respond.

He reached for her hand, and she was finally able to release a deep breath. She pulled in another and blew it out just as the elevator door slid open.

The reception room was classy and pristine, with all the usual pieces of furniture you'd expect, although a higher caliber. The reception desk gleamed their silhouettes back at them, and a chandelier cascaded down in long threads of light, secured by a polished silver chain nearly twenty feet above their heads. A quick appraisal of the creamy-white chairs, and a whiff of the pleasant fragrance of leather, had Abby convinced they were calfskin.

"May I help you?" A woman with perfectly smooth hair and skin looked back at them with the glimmer of a smile on her lips.

Chase glanced at Abby.

"Yes," she said, and even though she'd spoken quietly, it echoed in the open space. "I have an appointment, Abby Tanner?"

The woman's perfect eyebrows lifted. "Ah, yes. Abigail. You may have a seat."

"Thank you," Abby said, feeling some of her jitters

lessen from the small bit of conversation. But it didn't last long. In the next minute, they were called forward and directed through a door, down a hall, and into a small office. Part library, the room held a myriad of books along one wall, and a fire crackled warmly along the wall opposite.

Left alone to wait, Chase sat in a chair and Abby was browsing the titles when the door opened again. The man who joined them had dark, wavy hair and slender lips that seemed to stretch into nothingness when he smiled.

"Hello there, you must be Abigail." He shook her hand. "My name is Alan Jeffreys, and it's so nice to meet you. And this is?" His eyebrows rose in Chase's direction.

"My boyfriend, Chase," Abby answered.

"Hello," Chase smiled, looking completely at ease while shaking the man's hand.

"Please, have a seat," Mr. Jeffreys said, motioning to the chair next to Chase. Abby sat obediently, but her heart began to pound again.

"I do have some paperwork for you, although not as much as you'd think." He winked. "Since you've asked for your boyfriend to be present, we'll require a signature of confidentiality to include him. And these"—he handed them each a piece of paper—"are used to verify your identities. Go ahead and fill them out, and I'll hand them to my secretary while we discuss the particulars."

Abby filled out the top portion quickly but stopped when she got to the question of the closest relative. She fidgeted a little in her seat, feeling uncomfortable.

"What if I don't have a close relative?" she finally asked.

Mr. Jeffreys glanced up from the open briefcase on his desk. "No one?" he asked. Abby shrugged, not wanting to get into an explanation, but also knowing she'd have to be very honest with him. She caught Chase's eye briefly, and his quick smile was full of sympathy and understanding.

"Not even an aunt or uncle somewhere?"

"Well..." She shook her head. "I guess my father's brother would be the only one left. But he's so much older than my father, he has to be nearly ninety-five. I've only met him once when I was very young, so I'm not sure that's what you're looking for."

"No, that will be fine, I assure you." He nodded kindly. "Just write his name in, and we'll track down his information."

Abby nodded and finished filling out the paper.

"Thank you." Mr. Jeffreys opened a file and placed their two papers inside before pushing a button on his desk. They waited in silence while he pulled a few more papers and a book from the briefcase and closed it, shuffling the lock.

The office door opened, and he handed his secretary their file.

"Now." Mr. Jeffreys glanced at the door and waited until it had closed. "I am very confident in your identities. Those papers are just a formality, so what we're going to do is, start with the good stuff. When she comes back in, we can all act appropriately excited by the news that you are *you*." His eyes twinkled with mischief, and Abby couldn't help but laugh at his obvious enjoyment. She was beginning to like him very much.

He sobered when he looked down at the paper in his hands. "I'm sure you must have so many questions. I can't imagine the shock you must've felt at having received Sharalyn's letter. First, you need to understand, Sharalyn hired me to manage her final affairs, so I'm under contract to follow her wishes." He glanced back and forth between Chase and Abby. "It's not the way I would've handled it, I assure you. I gave her my advice, but in the end, it was her decision."

Abby nodded. "I understand."

"Okay, good." He straightened the paper with a flick. "Also, understand that while I wish she was here in person to have what, in my opinion, seems like a very necessary conversation, all I have is this letter that she wished me to read to you once you arrived in London." He glanced up briefly to see Abby nod again. "Well, here we go then. *My dearest niece.*" He glanced up, training his eyes on her pointedly.

Suddenly, Abby felt a reaching from the past into her heart. A communication with someone who cared deeply. A blood-relation who genuinely desired the best for her. It was a completely foreign feeling, and one she'd never known before. Warm and significant.

I know you have questions, but be pacified in knowing I have always wanted the very best for you. Your life has been difficult, and yet you've become a beautiful soul. I admire and love you for that." Mr. Jeffreys cleared his throat and read on. "*My relationship with your mother Ellen was a difficult one. I'm sure you guessed as much. But instead of leaving you to dig for information as to why, I have chosen to simply tell you myself. I hope beyond measure that you will find this information a comfort instead of a burden, my dear niece.*

Abby's heart was pounding again. She hadn't expected this. Her past was something she'd worked tremendously hard to rise above, and it wasn't a conversation easily shared with associates or even friends. Chase was the only person she'd openly trusted with it, and now he was looking back at her like he was afraid of what they would hear next. And if Abby was honest, she was afraid too.

But Mr. Jeffreys had only paused a moment before seeming to delve in.

When we were younger, we were very close, but the teenage years were hard on Ellen. Something happened inside her that became a crux in her life. She was hurting, but in those days, no one spoke of mental instability. It manifested in so many unpleasant ways, the least of which was the severing of our relationship. She blamed me for her struggles, and instead of allowing me to be of comfort, she shut me out of her life. As soon as she was able, she left our home and buried her problems deeper inside, hoping to leave her old self behind. But instead, her illness grew and strengthened, feeding on her fear and self-loathing. She managed to keep it at bay long enough to marry, but by the time she was blessed with you, it was clear there was a battle going on that she could no longer control. When she turned to addiction, I'm sure she had no other means of escape. I tell you this because it's something you should know. The mother you knew was a stranger to the real girl inside. The girl she was as a child. Warm and caring, giving to everyone. Indeed, she was a lot like you.

Abby's eyes burned; her throat closed. She fought to keep her composure, but her heart had been ripped from her chest. The mother that screamed, and abandoned, and shut herself away. The awful childhood she'd endured was the effect of an inner battle left unchecked. Never in her life had she considered this could be the case. She'd blamed the drugs and her mother's poor choices, but to suddenly see her from this angle was a tragedy she hadn't been ready for.

Her eyes were quickly welling up, and she tried to breathe quietly through her tears, wiping them away and blinking further moisture from her eyes.

Chase's hand had settled on her arm, but to look at him would mean losing it completely.

Mr. Jeffreys paused a moment and gave her a kind smile before continuing more gently.

If there was one thing I could change in my life, it would be to get Ellen to a doctor. One who would be able to understand and help her. I truly feel she did the best she could. My heart breaks for you and what you must have endured, but I couldn't let this truth about your mother die with me. I'm deeply sorry I was never allowed into your life. Your third birthday was the last time I saw you. Your dark curls were short and untamed and utterly beautiful. I held you and gave you a pink balloon. Perhaps you'll be able to find this memory buried inside. But even if it's lost, let me assure you my love does not diminish even from the gates of Heaven. I'm a determined woman and vow to watch over you for the duration of your life until we can meet again in the life beyond.

My deepest love, dear Bee,

Sharalyn

With a mighty breath, Mr. Jeffreys seemed to have usurped considerable strength. He held the letter in his hands, looking down at it for a moment in silence. When he did look up at Abby, she could see a hint of regret in his eyes.

"I apologize for this, Ms. Abigail, but again… I am to follow her wishes." He stood from his chair and walked to the fireplace, settling the fragile paper into the flames.

Abby flinched. She wanted to scream. To snatch it out of the flames and stomp them off each precious word. But she could only watch horrified as the page was quickly devoured, crumbling into ash amidst the deep blue belly of the fire.

CHAPTER 6

Chase had never seen such a haunted expression on Abigail before, as if she'd been thrown into the fire herself. He swallowed the tightness in his throat, working to calm the sudden overpowering emotion.

"I'm so sorry," Mr. Jeffreys repeated, returning to his chair. Abigail had yet to tear her eyes from the fire, and he waited politely, straightening a small leather book on the desk in front of him and stacking a few pages together.

When Abigail's gaze did finally wander back, he nodded softly. "Let's continue, if you please." He spoke quietly, as if guiding them carefully along a process he'd completed dozens of times before.

Chase admired his skill and compassion immensely.

"I know it's hard to lose something like that," Mr. Jeffreys said, "but hopefully this will be of some consolation." He handed Abby the leather-bound book. "This is a journal of Sharalyn's. She wanted you to have it."

Abby held the journal in her hands, gazing across the

cover. But she didn't open it. Instead, she set it carefully on her lap.

"And this"—Mr. Jeffreys held up two pages together—"is a writeup of everything Sharalyn possessed, and what she sold off. She didn't want anyone to be left with material possessions, besides the journal. So, she made sure it was all sold and consolidated into two separate accounts." He handed one page to Abigail and one to Chase. "These are copies, one for each of you. If you'll look across the top, this is the account that will be transferred into your name in the next few days."

Chase's mouth went dry as he gazed at the number. 1,000,000. It was a lot of zeros. He glanced at Abigail to see her face had frozen as well.

"It is an exceptional number, but you may notice it's not quite the amount we told you in our letter. And that's because of the second number. If you scan through all the chatter to the bottom... the second number brings you to a total of 200 million."

He stopped to sigh and lean back in his chair, glancing at the fire. "This second number is conditional, and will come to you in increments of 10 million per year... after you qualify for it."

Chase's head popped up at the same time as Abby's. He could see a hint of alarm on her features.

"Qualify for it?" she asked, looking back at Chase.

Chase winked and nodded his encouragement. Whatever it was, he was sure she could do it.

"Well." Mr. Jeffreys fiddled with the lock on his briefcase and opened it. "You're not exactly allowed to know the details. Your aunt had a great spirit for adventure.

You'll be given eight different challenges. After which, if completed, you will qualify for your inheritance. The first sum will be given immediately."

"But what if I can't do it?" Abigail asked.

Chase could see the stress on her features.

Mr. Jeffreys held a hand up. "Now, don't worry. I'm sure you'll be able to accomplish these, especially because of what's at stake." He was still looking into his briefcase, his eyes scanning across what Chase could only assume was a list of challenges. When he looked up again, he nodded. "Yes, you will. Don't worry, okay?"

Abigail sighed. "Okay," she mumbled.

The door opened, and the secretary walked in, smiling widely. She placed a paper on the desk and reached out for Abigail's hand, shaking it warmly, and then Chase's. "Congratulations," she said.

"Thank you," Chase answered. But Abigail remained silent. Her jitters and excitement had turned into something closer to despair.

They left the office soon after. Chase's thoughts were a blizzard of speculation and awe, and Abigail seemed to feel the same. Perhaps a little less exuberant. It wasn't until they were in their hotel suite that she finally let it out.

"I can't believe this," she groaned, walking to the window.

London was glittering with lights now, set inside a pale outline of cityscape.

"I have no idea what she's thinking, or what she has planned. And when did she even create these *challenges*? What if it's not possible to complete them anymore? What if the building she wants me to skydive off has been torn down?" She shook her head with a dry laugh at her reflection in the window.

It wasn't the way Chase had expected their day to end. He'd pictured himself taking her out to celebrate somewhere exclusive and ridiculously expensive. "I know it's not what you'd expected, but Abby..." He waited for her to look up from the chaise lounge she'd slumped into. "You've just inherited a million dollars. That's incredible!"

Her lips lifted from their downward pull. She rested on one elbow, nodding thoughtfully. "It is incredible, don't get me wrong. It's just... you know me."

She rolled her eyes at herself, and although Chase thought he knew exactly where her conversation was headed, he waited for her to continue.

"The second I went from wanting that house, to realizing I might be able to get it, I let myself go crazy with the possibilities." She sighed. "One million isn't enough. And what if it's sold before I can complete these silly challenges and get the rest?"

Chase nodded back at her. The fact that she was reasoning with herself lifted his spirits. Maybe she would back out on the house without him having to suggest it. With how the inheritance was tied up, he couldn't imagine her taking such a big risk without the cash on hand.

"There's no point in worrying about it now, just try to let it go. Take it step by step," he said. "Time will often reveal things in ways that are otherwise impossible. Just give it a little time."

"Hmm," she mused, "I like that."

He used to hold back his more Yoda-style advice from people, sure it was too flowery and abstract. But it just seemed to flow from him naturally, and when he met Abigail, she'd been thrilled with his habit of poetic advice. He'd never felt more free to be himself... and he'd never been so shocked to find out that someone could adore it.

She was still smiling at him, and he joined her on the chaise lounge, gathering her in his arms and enjoying the way she wrapped herself into his embrace. Their relationship had been close like this for nearly a year, and Chase couldn't imagine ever being apart.

In the beginning, when he had trouble turning off his therapist's mind, he'd been worried about her. The way she constantly looked for something new—something better. She went from one job to the next, and Chase feared she would someday trade him in for a newer, shinier version. He'd counseled enough patients with the very same problem, and they rarely stayed with their partners for more than a few months. Not one of them made it to a year.

And yet here they were, approaching a year and still very much in love. He tried to swallow the doubt away completely, telling himself that he'd misjudged her. The rough childhood she'd been raised with had left its scars, but perhaps this wasn't one of them. He had a sudden thought of the ring he'd wanted to buy her. A brilliant fairy-tale diamond. He'd been so close, but that was the day she'd admitted she didn't like her job, that she wanted something new. And he'd lost his nerve. But now he wished he had it in his pocket.

"You're right, of course," Abigail said, lifting her head

to kiss him. "I guess I was just so set on rushing forward with everything. Thank you so much for understanding." She smiled with an energy that glowed in her cheeks. "Should we go get something to eat?"

CHAPTER 7

They'd been home nearly a week, and Abby had hardly seen Chase for a few minutes. His double workload was a result of their last-minute trip to London. Abby loved him for that—she could always count on him. And the way he'd soothed her about the house at Poppyridge Cove, when she felt so lost, had allowed an idea to sprout in her mind.

She stood at the same realty office of the man she'd first spoken to about it. He seemed to know quite a lot about the property, so he was a natural choice.

His black eyebrows lifted in recognition when he saw Abby. She brought her hand up in a small wave.

"You," he said, surprised. "Well, hello again. Abigail Tanner, is it?" he glanced down at an appointment book.

"Yes, that's right. We spoke at the sourdough bread store."

"I remember." He nodded cheerily. "What can I do for you?"

"Well." Abby rubbed her hands together, feeling

nervous. "I would like to purchase the property, but I don't know if my idea will work. I want to run it by you first."

"Okay," he encouraged, nodding and clasping his hands together.

"I've, uh, inherited a bit of money, although it isn't enough. I'll be receiving more, but not for another eight months." She twisted her bag in her hands. "What I'm wondering is, would I be able to secure a loan on the premise of receiving this additional inheritance in the future? With the one million I have, I thought maybe half of that could go toward a down payment, and the other half could be used to begin repairs?"

She paused, waiting for him to jump in at some point. But he seemed to still be thinking it over. His sleek black hair was pushed back uniformly and sat as still as the rest of him. She fidgeted, opening her mouth to continue.

"Yes," he said quietly.

Her mouth hung for a moment, and she repeated that little word in her head. "I'm sorry?" she asked, not sure which of her ramblings he was referring to. She hoped it was yes to everything, but how could he grant her all of that after almost no discussion? Didn't he want to check out her story first?

"Yes," he repeated, standing and walking the length of his office with his hands held behind his back.

He was much taller than she remembered, but perhaps that was because she was sitting down. She wondered if she should be standing too.

"Yes, you would be able to secure the loan you need and use the other half to begin repairs. That's a very good offer—one I'm fairly certain they would accept."

THE SECRET OF POPPYRIDGE COVE

His words were saying yes, but his expression was saying no. His face was solemn, and he turned to gaze out the window in silence.

"So, I can go ahead and make an offer?" she asked quietly, confused by his silence.

He sighed deeply before turning back to her, and his intense gaze seemed to hold her by the throat. She swallowed.

"Yes, technically you *can*. But do you *want* to? *Should* you? I can honestly say, I don't know how to advise you on this. It's a unique situation. One I've never found myself in before. Such a beautiful property, like none I've ever seen… but whatever's going on there…" His gaze was prying as if he could stare into her soul to find the answer.

"I understand that," Abby said, speaking carefully. She didn't want to undervalue his warning, but she'd already thought over the shocking sight at the house. "But really, I believe this is just a case of an abandoned house being used as a secret place. Once we begin visiting the grounds and cleaning things up, I'm sure there won't be any more problems. Whatever creature is coming around, it will find a new, more isolated area."

She nodded back at him, sure he would agree with her. Any rational person would. What other view was there? It was simple.

He took a breath, relenting his stillness with a nod. But he remained silent and began to pace, gazing out the window from time to time. Abby began to feel a bit irritated. Why wasn't he moving on with the paperwork? Was he not taking her seriously? What if someone else made an offer while they were just sitting around *discussing*?

"Okay," he finally said, although he continued his pacing. "Let's make an offer. But I want to add a condition that the property be cleaned of any unpleasant refuse, and we're given an inspection date where we can personally inspect the property before finalizing." He turned back to her, finally stilling his feet.

Abby couldn't believe it. Her head was spinning with anticipation, with the idea that she—Abigail Tanner—could ever own a property like that. Balanced at the coast's edge, surrounded by redwoods.

Her throat felt suddenly thick. She wanted to share it with everyone. Every child who'd ever known their family's lowly place on the economic ladder. Every young couple who'd searched for the perfect romantic escape. Every grandparent who wished for tranquility with the world around them.

She knew then what she was going to do. An inn that would be a nod to old world values and loaded with the clean lines and luxurious fabrics of modern décor, plus her personal style and flavor. It felt like an other-worldly guiding hand was brushing aside any other possibilities for her in life except for this one. And with such support from the universe, she couldn't fail.

Her gaze lifted to Mr. Craig, and she straightened her back.

"Perfect."

* * *

S̶ʜᴇ ᴡᴀs ᴡᴀɪᴛɪɴɢ at Chase's townhouse when he returned home from work. It was late, nearly 8:30 p.m. But his weary face lifted to a smile when he saw Abby. Her adrenaline had never calmed since she'd signed the papers, and she doubted she'd be able to sleep that night. Or ever again.

Thank you, Sharalyn.

"Are you hungry?" she asked, glad when Chase shook his head. She couldn't hold her excitement in any longer.

"No, thanks. I ate at work." He paused to eye her, likely noticing some key differences in the color of her cheeks and arch of her eyebrows. "What's up?" he finally asked, letting a smile find its way through his exhaustion.

"Well…" Abby grabbed his arm and towed him to the living room, where they sat on the couch together. She was so glad it was Friday. Maybe they could drive out to Poppyridge in the morning. Just to give it another look.

"I went to Vance Craig's office today, just to talk about the house. I haven't been able to stop thinking about it, especially after our conversation in London."

She grinned, but Chase's expression was perplexed. She only half noticed.

"So, I spoke to him about splitting the one million I have, making an offer with half and using the other half to start on renovations while I wait for the rest—and he agreed!"

"Whoa." Chase woke a bit, leaning forward. "Hold on. You already did this?"

"Yes!" she cheered. "Well, we sent the offer. I'm hoping we hear back tomorrow. Can you believe it, Chase? Should we drive out and look around tomorrow?" Her excitement was bubbling over so fiercely she felt close to tears, but Chase had yet to crack a smile. Instead, he continued to look shocked.

"And who's Vance Craig again?" he asked, sounding entirely too calm.

Abby's hands came to her hips. "The realtor. The one we spoke to in the bread store."

"Ah. Yes, I remember."

Chase glanced up at her, and his eyes still lacked the excitement she was looking for. A bit of irritation pricked at her heart.

"I…" He rubbed his neck with one hand. "I didn't mean for you to jump in like this. I thought maybe you'd complete the challenges first and then pursue it after you were allocated the inheritance. Are you prepared to take on a two-million-dollar loan? That just seems… I don't know, doesn't that make you nervous?"

A deep hole formed in Abby's stomach, and her excitement was sinking into it. She began to feel like a fool, the way he stated it. Two million dollars. Was she crazy? In an instant, she turned back into a little girl with stained clothes and a bruise on her cheek from an intoxicated mother who'd lost her temper. But Abby's memories were crystal clear, and she hated how quickly she felt pushed back into the box she grew up in.

She thought, for one glorious moment, that she could be seen as something else—renovate an inn like none other and share it with *the world*. But she was back to being the little girl with hardly a penny… and a two-million-dollar loan was suddenly a complete joke.

She sank back into the couch, staring at the coffee table and cursing her eyes until they stopped stinging.

"Maybe I should wait," she said, trying her best to sound unaffected. But she was crushed.

"Bee, I didn't mean to make you feel bad. It's just a bit of a shock, that's all. I'm not saying you shouldn't—"

"It's late." Abby stood. "I should head home." She walked to the door, and Chase followed right beside her, dodging a chair and accent table along the way.

"I'm just saying, that's a big decision," he persisted. "That's all. I'm not saying you can't do it. I'm sorry if I pushed you into it at first. The whole prospect was just so exciting, I guess I got carried away."

She stopped at the door, holding her hand up. "I know, I know. It's a big decision, and really, I did rush into it. I'll give you a call tomorrow, and we can talk about it, okay? I'm just tired, and my house is a disaster."

He shifted on his feet, and Abby could see he knew she was just escaping. With a sigh, he relented. "Okay... let me walk you to your car? It's dark out."

* * *

THE NIGHT STRETCHED on with Abby grumbling to herself in her empty apartment. It wasn't a mess. In fact, it was sparkling clean, not even a dish in the sink. But she hadn't wanted to fall apart in front of Chase. He already knew enough about her childhood, and his therapist's mind could always perfectly match the reason behind her every feeling. It irritated her. Like she was standing naked in front of the mirror. She didn't want him to know so much about her insecurities.

She just wanted him to trust her, for once. Not see her as the dependent one. Although, she did depend on him...

CHAPTER 8

Vance's car was a new crossover, clean inside and capable on the roads. She'd never turned off the highway at the exit he took before. It was a small, one-lane road that took them through fields and hills. An occasional house could be seen nestled between trees here and there, and by the looks of them, they were mostly farmhouses... and a few mansions. The rich who only knew about this area by flying over it in their private jets. It seemed very private and perfectly nostalgic.

They turned uphill, onto a road lined with grown trees. Their slender trunks were uniform and tall, and the leaves had begun to change to a brilliant shade of red. An old fence trailed along one side, built long ago. Abby recognized it as matching the one she'd seen up at the house, and she wondered for the first time just how much the property might encompass.

"Is this part of it?" she asked, still gazing into what had become the edge of the redwood forest. The ocean was bound to show itself on the other side of the road, but so far it was still fields of crops and cattle.

Vance looked very relaxed, smiling out at their surroundings. "This used to be a private road to the residence, but since the small development was built at the end here, it's now an access for them as well. Your property begins just beyond those houses." He smiled at her as he said that last part as if he knew how it would burn in her chest.

My property. Abby leaned closer to her window, catching sight of a new fence line and the top of a house.

"There's a total of twenty acres at the Poppyridge house. Did you know that?" he turned to Abby with the question.

"Oh." She shook her head. "I didn't realize there was so much land attached to it. That's incredible."

"And there's private access to Poppyridge Cove right off the back porch." Vance slowed, coming up on a neighbor standing by his mailbox. An older man Abby guessed to be at least 80. He smiled and raised a hand as they passed.

"We could stop and say hello if you'd like," Vance suggested. "Might be good to get a feel of the area, meeting a few neighbors."

Abby was still craning to see farther down the road, but it curved out of sight. "Maybe on the way back?" she asked. The idea of waiting any longer was torture.

Vance chuckled, turning back to the road. "Okay, deal. Mr. Fillmore is the man we just passed. He's lived out here for a long time. He and his wife, although she passed away some years ago."

Abby glanced back, just catching sight of him again

before he was out of view. He seemed so pleasant and kind, it was sad to think of him alone.

"And this second house is a vacation property. The family is very energetic and kind. They've had me out for a couple BBQs back when they were thinking of selling. But now they rotate the property between the ten siblings, splitting the cost and letting everyone enjoy it."

"Ten siblings?" Abby gawked, turning around to admire the tall, stately cabin. It fit well surrounded by pines.

"It's a blended family," Vance explained, "but they get along very well. Probably better than most, I'd say."

"Hmm," Abby commented, agreeing with him quietly.

"The next two I know are inhabited, but I've only seen the families here and there. I've never met them. Smaller families with just a few kids who are nearly grown. This next one is a rental, and the last house in the row is owned by a very wealthy colonel in the Army. Or, retired colonel I should say. His flag is always flying." He gestured to the flagpole with the red, white, and blue colors waving at the top. It looked crisp and new.

"Sounds like a nice group." Abby glanced behind them as they passed the colonel's house. "I can't wait to meet them all." But her excitement to meet the neighbors was nothing compared to the awakening growing inside of her as they wound up the last hill. A wide space opened up in front of them.

The house came into view at the same time as the cliff's edge did, and the ocean beyond that. It couldn't have been better placed in any possible way. The grand front of the house had what looked to be an old fountain at one time, balancing out the face of the property. It was stained and cracked, but still beautiful.

Vance pulled up alongside the house on the ocean side. His car crept slowly forward until Abby could just begin to see around to the back porch. "Stop." She grabbed Vance's arm, and the car jerked to a stop. Her heart had begun to pound with the memories of what she'd seen before, and the horrid smell of it all. She glanced around them, back to the road where they'd come, and deep into the trees. Searching.

"Hey." Vance placed his hand over hers, and she jumped.

"I'm sorry," she said, releasing her grip. She hadn't realized how tightly she'd grabbed him. There was nearly a handprint on the fabric of his suit shirt. "It was just…"

She looked back into his face, wondering if he'd seen the back deck before. And had it been littered with animals? "When I first came here, it was a mess in the back." She glanced between his eyes, not wanting to say more.

But he seemed to understand. He nodded solemnly. "I've heard of the dead animals that keep showing up here, Abby. We don't have to get out if you don't want to. We can always wait until the property is ready for your final inspection."

Abby let out a breath, working to steady her shaking hands. "No, that's okay. I want to look around."

"Okay." He placed his hand on her shoulder. "Stay here and let me take a look first."

She was embarrassed for making such a big deal over it but found herself nodding back at him and feeling a rush of gratitude that she wasn't alone.

She watched Vance get out.

He smiled back at her and walked to the edge of the house, disappearing around the back. The two seconds that he was out of sight had her heart racing again, imagining the horrors he could be facing. She jumped when he appeared again.

He smiled widely and waved her forward. "It's okay," he called.

Her ridiculous fears had quickly managed to explode when left on their own; she stepped out of the car with a sigh.

The first breath of ocean and redwoods brought everything back that she'd fallen in love with. It was like a memory of her childhood. Like déjà vu, only she'd never experienced anything like it as a child. Maybe it had been in her dreams. Some magical land she knew never existed in real life. Except now, she was here.

She walked the length of the house, catching up to Vance and trying not to cringe as she turned the corner to the back of the property. The deck was completely clear of the wreckage that had covered it before, and she sighed another breath of relief.

"The door should've been left open," Vance said. His eyes were sparkling with excitement, and he marched up the wooden stairs. His footsteps sounded solid and warm, like the house was glad to have company.

Abby lingered at the bottom, sure it was locked. Why would a mansion like this be left open?

He turned the handle and pushed the door open. "Looks like we're in luck." He grinned back at her.

She rushed up the steps, walking through and gazing up at the light streaming in through the windows, leaving perfectly crossed patterns on the wood floors and banisters. Dust was caked throughout, and their footsteps were the only ones. Like treading on newly fallen snow.

"Has no one come inside?" she asked, awed by the open spaces and beautifully elegant chandeliers. Through glass French doors, she could see a dazzling ballroom with a patterned floor and molded ceiling. It was incredible, beyond what she ever hoped.

"No, I don't believe so," Vance answered quietly, sliding his hand along the banister and glancing up the stairs. "I don't think anyone's gotten this far."

"It's gorgeous," Abby breathed, walking the length of the house to the grand front doors. Tall and solid with a rustic white finish, all she'd have to do is hang wreaths, and they'd be a Christmas postcard. Through the long windows next to the doors, she could see the fountain. She imagined it restored and lit up, light sparkling through the cascading water.

"Do you want to see upstairs?" Vance asked.

She turned to see him standing aside the beautiful stairway.

"Yes," she walked back slowly, admiring what she could see of the kitchen and a sitting room as she passed. The stairs seemed in decent shape, a squeak here and there, but not anything too horrendous. For the most part, she was amazed at the state the house was in. It seemed strong and beautiful. How had it been left unpurchased for so long?

There were seven bedrooms upstairs, with five smaller and two with a more generous, master-bedroom feel. The hallway was open on one side with a banister giving them a beautiful view into the kitchen and great room.

Through high narrow windows, they could see the redwoods on one side and the coastline on the other.

"It's incredible," Abby said, hardly able to believe it.

"It's absolutely incredible," Vance repeated, as lost in the place as she was. He tapped one hand on the banister. "Do you want to see the cove?"

Abby's gaze flickered back to him, and a smile stretched across her face. "I almost forgot about that."

They followed their footprints back outside, with Abby holding her breath across the deck, afraid of smelling any reminders to what had been there before. But nothing was tainting the air aside from the sea, the pine, and the hundreds of brilliant orange poppies. They sprouted up about halfway down the small access path. It was bordered on one side by a rope, strung along between frequent posts.

Abby's hand hovered over it, sliding across the weathered rope here and there, and resting atop the sun-warmed wood. The pathway was sandy, and while not exactly steep, it did require them to pay attention to their feet.

When they reached the bottom, Abby's toes finally sunk into the deeper sand of the cove. She pulled her sandals off and stepped through the sand. A shallow warm layer sunk into cold, deeper layers. It was refreshing and wild. Untouched. The hill behind them protected them from the wind and captured the warmth of the sun. Beyond their access path, the cliffside became steep and rocky, littered with tide pools and archways. Even the deep hollow of a cave could be seen far beyond.

It was a coastline Abby could spend weeks exploring. She couldn't stop herself from smiling. Not even a little.

Vance glanced back at her and grinned, and she shook her head. "I still can't believe it." She laughed, gazing again at the ocean glittering through small patches of fog. "This is more than I ever imagined."

She turned to Vance again, and her excitement settled into a sincere gratitude. "Thank you so much."

He dipped his head. "My pleasure."

Their walk back up the path was humbling, with both of them huffing by the time they reached the top. Vance held his hand out, guiding Abby up the last few steps. She smiled. "Thank—" Her eyes caught something gray stretched out on the deck, and even from where they stood, she could see a dark liquid dripping off the wood.

"Vance!" She gasped, holding on to him and searching the forest for anyone. Anything.

His head whipped around, and he held his arm around her. "Oh my—" He looked into the woods, pulling Abby with him as he rushed toward his car. Abby could make out the animal on the porch. Long fur and ringed tail. A raccoon.

A crackling of twigs and brush had them both skirting to the side. Vance stepped in front of her and held one arm out as if warding off an attack. "Keep going," he urged.

Abby held on to him, pulling him with her. "You too."

They hurled themselves into his car, closing the doors and locking them. Vance twisted his keys and jerked the gear shift into reverse a little too quickly. The car lurched and died. He pushed it back into park and tried again. They were both breathing hard, still searching the trees as he backed out and sped down the street.

"Maybe you can meet the neighbors another time," Vance said, finally stilling his breath.

Abby didn't answer. She closed her eyes and concentrated on calm, steady breaths. It wasn't until Vance placed his hand over hers that she finally managed to calm the shaking.

"I'm sorry, Abby," he said. "But I think we should call the police."

She looked into his eyes, shocked. Why did her dream have to come wrapped in a nightmare? But he was right, she knew it. She couldn't just hope whatever was killing these animals would stop simply because she bought the place. It was so twisted, though. What was the point of it? What did it mean?

She pulled her phone from her bag and dialed 911, and Vance came to a stop at the side of the road. He listened with her as the line connected.

"Yes," Abby said. "I believe it's an emergency, but I'm not sure. I've just purchased this property, and dead animals keep showing up on the porch..." She stopped as the woman cut her off. "No, not animal control. They're dead animals. Beheaded. It must have just happened—" She bit her lip and suddenly felt completely foolish as the woman lectured her on what was considered an emergency. "Okay, I will. Thank you." She hung up and turned back to Vance. "I guess the local police department is my next call."

"Okay," he said, glancing across the street at the few homes in view. "Maybe I'll just talk to a few neighbors while you do that... see if they've heard anything."

She nodded back at him while listening to a police officer's greeting. "Yes, sorry to bother you," she began, not wanting another lecture. "I've just purchased a home that's been abandoned for years, and I came out to take a look at it. But dead animals keep showing up on the porch. One was just killed a few minutes ago—"

"Is this the Poppyridge place?" the officer asked.

"Uh—yes. Do you know what's going on?"

"I'll send a car out, ma'am. Please wait for them at the property."

Abby cringed. "We'll be down the street from the property if that's okay."

He agreed, although Abby was sure she could hear a smile in the officer's voice as he said goodbye. It set her off a bit. Just what was so funny? What if a bear was prowling the woods? One that had developed a thirst for killing? Or a wolf? They could have been attacked.

She shivered, looking out the windows and into the woods. Dark and mysterious. Would she really be comfortable living here? Especially when there could be some wild creature at large? She bit her lip, trying to imagine herself walking off into the trees alone. It had never bothered her before, but now the thought had her chest tightening in fear.

The car door opened, and she turned quickly with an intake of breath, just managing to smooth out the surprise on her face before Vance leaned down to talk to her.

"What did they say?" he asked.

"They're sending a car out."

"Good." He tilted his head across the street. "Gives us just enough time for lunch. Would you like to meet the Allens?"

Abby managed a smile, and as they walked across the

road, her stomach finally settled just enough to feel an immense hunger.

The Allen's home could easily be featured in a magazine. The moment she'd entered, Abby's eyes had been drawn to the incredible view. From the inside, it was more of a cabin than a modern home, although still chic. Long, stacked rectangular windows gave a full view of the hillside of trees, their pine tops bunched together in a deep green huddle.

"Your home is beautiful," she complimented, glancing at the strong-jawed general and Mrs. Allen with her delicate features and silky brown hair. They both smiled their thanks.

"Now, Mr. Craig here was telling me you'd had another animal left at your place?" The general asked.

Abby nodded. "Yes, just while we were down at the beach. It couldn't have been more than thirty minutes that we were away from the house. Have you heard anything?"

They shook their heads together, looking very in sync. "No dear," Mrs. Allen answered. "I'm afraid not. Although, about a week ago the smell had gotten so bad that I called the neighbors, and we each contacted the police department to complain. That seemed to fix the problem."

She brushed her feathery hair back with a swish of one hand.

"But my goodness, if it's just going to continue, something needs to be done. People will start moving out."

"How long have you lived here?" Abby asked as plates were placed around the table. Deli-style sandwiches were atop each one, loaded with layers of meat, cheese, and lettuce.

The general held the last plate, settling it in front of

Vance. "Five years now. We were the first ones to move in. It was so different when we were the only house. Felt like we owned the whole mountain." He smiled at the memory, glancing at his wife. "'Course, no one ever lived in the Poppyridge place, although I admit we snuck through the grounds now and then to access the cove. It's a beautiful piece of coastline."

Abby swallowed her last bite of turkey and provolone. "It's gorgeous," she echoed.

A knock sounded at the door. Loud and official.

"They're here," Vance said, waiting for Abby.

She turned to the Allens. "Thank you so much for lunch. It was delicious."

"You're very welcome," Mrs. Allen beamed. "I hope we become neighbors."

The policeman at the door was hardly as neighborly. He didn't crack a smile and rattled off something as he read from a paper on his clipboard. It sounded very much like Abby's complaint had been scribbled down word for word.

"Okay ma'am, let's take a look," he grumbled as if he'd rather be doing anything else in the city.

"It's at the end of the road here," Abby pointed, heading to Vance's car.

"Yes, I know where it is," the officer answered. He started his car and made a wide U-turn, heading to the property.

Vance lifted his eyebrows at Abby, and they followed behind. The officer didn't waste time circling the house. The moment he stepped from his squad car, he was off on a mission, taking notes and finally stopping at the back patio. He'd stopped writing.

"And this wasn't here when you arrived the first time?" he asked, directing his question at Abby. She glanced around, looking into the woods briefly. "No." She looked up at him. "We'd found the house open and went inside, and from there, we walked down to the beach. When we came back up, it was here. Just like this. We never saw another animal, although we did hear something in the bushes."

The officer's gaze shot back up to Abby, and he peered into her eyes for a moment. "Another animal?" he finally asked.

"Er, yes," Abby flustered, "we don't know what killed this raccoon."

"I'm sorry, ma'am, but you have the wrong idea. This animal was killed by a person. I'm positive about that."

Abby's heart sunk, and a cold breeze touched her neck. What did he mean a person did it? "So, you're saying while we were at the beach, someone killed this raccoon and left it here? Why would they do that?"

He shook his head, still writing on his notepad.

"You're sure?" Vance asked, taking a moment to study their surroundings again.

"Yes, sir. I'm positive," the officer repeated. "Knew as much when we had them clean up the last group of carcasses. But the property owner is very responsive, got right to it when the neighbors started complaining about the smell. I'll let them know you'd like them to come out again." He touched the brim of his hat like he was preparing to leave.

Abby held a hand up. "Wait, that's it?" she asked, "You're not going to... I don't know, launch an investigation or something? Question people?"

He held his arms out, looking around. "And who do you propose I question?" he asked. "The neighbors? Because they've all been very bothered by this, I assure you. Each one has called in and complained profusely."

"So, don't you want to know what's going on? Isn't it your responsibility to figure this out? To keep us safe?" Abby knew she should've stopped, but the questions just kept coming. What was he thinking by just leaving them here without any answers? It was infuriating.

"Ma'am, let me assure you of your safety. Unless you happen to be a small forest creature, you've got nothing to worry about. Probably just someone's idea of a joke. They'll give it up when they realize someone's movin' in." He touched his hat again, more decidedly this time, like he wasn't happy that she kept him here longer than he'd planned.

"Okay," she finally relented, wishing things had gone differently. She wanted a full investigation. Officers by the dozen sweeping the forest and searching out clues. But with a large city like San Francisco nearby, she figured they had a lot more pressing calls to follow up on.

She took a deep breath, leaning her back against a patio pillar, and watched as the squad car disappeared from view.

CHAPTER 9

When they got back to Vance's car and began their drive home, they were both lost in thought. Abby felt something vibrate next to her ankle and reached into her purse to find she'd missed a call from Chase. And a text. And another call. She hesitated, sure it would be awkward talking to Chase about everything while Vance was listening in. She decided to call him as soon as she got home. His text was just a quick hello anyway, nothing urgent.

"Well, this didn't turn out quite like we'd thought, did it?" Vance asked, glancing at her briefly before turning his gaze back to the road. They'd reached the highway again, and traffic was congested in the late afternoon.

"No, it didn't." Abby felt more discouraged than she wanted to admit. She continued studying passing cars, not feeling in the mood for a conversation.

"That was a pretty shocking sight," Vance continued. "I keep imagining who might have done that while we were at the beach. And why? That's the question I keep coming back to. Why?"

Abby sighed. "I don't know. It doesn't make any sense."

"It can't be directed at you, because it's been happening for six months at least. So, who would they be trying to scare off with those dead animals?"

Vance's pondering was starting to grate on Abby. She didn't want to hear it anymore. Her happily ever after was becoming tainted, and she wished it would fade from her memory. Analyzing it to pieces was hardly helpful. But Vance kept going on and on about the Allens, and the rental house next door to them, and the old man who'd looked so kind.

"Why don't you just set up a camera?" he finally asked, turning to her.

"I don't want to talk about it anymore," Abby blurted out. "Wait, what?" she asked, turning to face him. "A camera?"

Vance had one eyebrow raised and had taken his eyes off the road long enough for Abby to glance at it for him. "Was I bothering you?" he finally asked, returning his gaze to the street.

"Oh." Abby twisted her hands together. Why would he care if he was bothering her anyway? "No, you weren't. I'm sorry, I didn't mean to be rude. It's just still such a shock. I wish I didn't have to worry about it."

He nodded, although he didn't look at her again. "That's understandable. But if you think about it, the only reason the house hasn't sold in this market is because of those animals. It's really what has given you this opportunity. So, a blessing in disguise maybe?"

"Yeah, you might be right about that," she said, taking the time to glance over his face. His skin was a pleasant color, rich and warm. It went perfectly with his black hair. And as tall as he was, it gave him a very Clark Kent look.

He glanced over, catching her staring. Her cheeks immediately felt warm, and she dropped her gaze, wishing she had more control over her heart. It raced away, mistaking her surprise for something else.

"We're here," he said quietly, pulling up to the curb alongside her apartment.

Abby looked around, unaware that they'd already made it back. "Oh, thank you," she said, snatching her bag from the floor and trying to avoid looking at Vance again. Her cheeks were bound to be red, and he would read all the wrong messages from that.

But he touched her arm, and she turned back to him. "Wait," he said, more quietly than he needed to. "I'm sorry if I made light of what happened today. You're perfectly justified in being shocked. Just remember you're not in a contract yet. You have every right to step out of this until the final inspection date in ten days. Then you'll have to decide."

Abby let her breath out, realizing her fears had been misplaced. He was just being professional.

"Thank you," she smiled, "that does help."

He dropped his hand from her arm only to have his fingertips trace her hand and softly clasp it in his.

"I'm glad," he said. "Goodbye, Abby."

Her stomach coiled into knots and turned slowly to sickness. What did he mean by holding her hand? She stepped out of the car and looked up to see Chase standing at her door. He nodded back at Vance, and Abby turned back to him as well, giving herself time to relax as she watched him drive away.

She didn't know if Chase had seen Vance take her hand. His expression didn't *look* betrayed, but she *felt* like it had been an utter betrayal. She tried to wipe it from her features as she walked up the steps but could hardly manage a smile.

Chase stood tall and confident with a gentle grin on his face. It was what she'd first noticed about him. His smile belonged on a cover model, and she'd seen the way people stopped when they noticed it too. Especially women. He'd laughed when she suggested he not smile at his patients, but for their sake and his, she knew she was right. It was disarming on so many levels.

She felt her throat tighten, and tears threatened to sting her eyes. But Chase didn't notice. He seemed lost in his thoughts. "Was that the realtor?" He waited after she'd nodded like he wanted her to say more.

But Abby wasn't sure quite where to start. It had been such a rollercoaster, from the house to Vance… She reached for the door. "Are you hungry?" She felt immediately guilty since she'd only asked to ward off any remarks about her day.

And food was something Chase was passionate about. He chatted about sandwiches, pasta, and soups until they made it to the second floor and into her apartment.

"I'll make it," Chase said cheerfully, taking her bag from her shoulder and setting it on the counter. "You really look tired."

Abby felt sick again. But she knew what would make her feel better. "Thanks." She reached for his hand, stopping him in mid-dinner prep. "Can we talk for just a minute before you get started?"

"Oh." Chase stood with a bowl he'd taken from the cupboard. He set it on the counter over a burn mark. "Sure, no problem."

They settled on the couch, and Abby told him about going to Poppyridge. His expression at first didn't look very happy, but soon he was smiling with her as she described the interior of the house and the cove. She hesitated to tell the rest, but her stomach was still twisting. "But when we walked back up from the beach, there was a dead raccoon on the porch."

"What?" Chase had nearly jumped from his seat, and his grip had tightened on her hand. "Did you see what killed it?"

"No, we didn't see anything. We called the police, and he said it…" She paused, wishing she didn't have to finish. The look in Chase's eyes was panicked enough. "He said it was a person who'd been doing this. Not an animal." She nodded before he could ask. "He was positive."

That seemed to stop him completely, and his gaze wandered over her apartment. "A person…" he mumbled, finally turning back to her. "So, what now? What are they going to do?"

"They'll have the company clean it up." She shrugged, wishing there was more.

"That's it?" Chase threw his hands in the air. "What if this person's insane? I mean, obviously, they are, but what if they're dangerous?"

Abby sighed. "Well, the officer seemed to think only small forest creatures were at risk. I guess they don't put much stock in those." The more she thought over his response, the angrier she became. "Maybe I'll call the police station again."

Chase shook his head, and one hand settled on her shoulder. "Let me." He waited until Abby agreed, and then with a breath, it seemed all over.

He stood and pulled her up into his arms. "I'm glad you're okay," he whispered, kissing her quickly. "I wish I could have been there with you." His eyes asked the question he hadn't, and he paused, looking back at her as if the answer might be written on her face.

And Abby worried that it was. Her heart had begun beating again like it meant to blackmail her completely. "I just wanted to be sure about the house first," she explained, "before I talked to you about it. I know you don't like the idea."

He nodded. "You're right, I don't. And now I especially don't. At first it seemed so easy, and then we learned about Aunt Sharalyn's deal, and it quickly became more complicated than I'm comfortable with. But I'm not the one buying it, you are. So was your trip worth it?"

She looked up into his hazel eyes, a bit stunned. "What?"

"You said you weren't sure. So… are you?" He walked to the kitchen while he waited for her answer, and she mulled it over as deeply as she could in the few seconds that passed.

Anyone else would run. She knew that. It was a terrifying thought, that someone was killing animals and leaving them at the house she wanted to buy. What did that even mean? But there was no mistaking the way she felt the moment she'd entered the beautiful building. It invited her in, warmly wrapped her in its arms with visions of Christmas parties and joyous vacations. Garland and lights. A crackling fire. Old and new friends. Things she should have experienced as a child, but all they'd ever been were dreams. Dreams that she wanted to make come true.

"I'm buying it."

Chase fumbled with the knife he held, and it clattered to the counter. "Abby," he said sternly, waiting for her to continue and perhaps hoping she would take it back.

But she wasn't going to. She gazed at him, settled in her decision, and wished he'd be the one to surrender.

"Okay," he said stiffly, continuing to slice vegetables and sprinkle them over a leafy green salad.

They didn't speak much the rest of the night, except to comment on the food. It pricked at Abby's heart to know he was so set against this decision. To her, it was the first miracle she'd ever experienced. Something she'd stumbled upon in the woods—or been led to. She'd begun to think the latter was more accurate.

What else would explain it? To find the house and then suddenly be granted a way to purchase it. It was incredible, beyond anything she could have imagined. Why couldn't he see that?

When their dinner was finished and the polite conversation had faded, he stood at her doorway, waiting through a heavy silence.

Just as he turned to go, he stopped and faced her again, sighing deeply. "I don't want you to do this. And if you want me to speak honestly, I'd have to say I'm shocked that you're still considering it. That's a lot of money, Bee."

He looked up from the floor, and her heart sunk a little.

Chase pulled off his shirt and twisted the shower handle, letting the water heat up. He watched his reflection in the mirror as steam began to tint the edges and swirl through the middle.

But what if he was wrong? He rubbed his tired eyes, thinking of the small piece of jewelry he'd finally bought and hidden in his dresser drawer. His heart pounded at the thought of giving it to her, followed swiftly by various options of how she might react. If indeed she was running from her happily ever after, it would be a green light for her to dump him. Dump him and run.

Then again... maybe she already had.

He looked back at the mirror, now only a slight shadow behind a thick layer of steam. Fading away. Maybe for good this time.

"Great job, jerk," he mumbled, wiping one hand across the mirror and leaving only streaks of reflection staring back at him.

* * *

THE WEEKEND BEGAN with a long list of tasks Chase had been meaning to get to for over a month. He repaired two bathroom faucets and a dresser drawer, fertilized and trimmed his lawn, and finally moved into the garage, determined to organize every box, hiking boot, and stray ski. And his mind had been given the freedom to wander while he'd been rushing around.

He thought over the house at Poppyridge—still convinced it was an exceptionally bad idea—and every avenue he could think of that would explain the refuse

But maybe he was wrong.

He started down the stairs.

Maybe she didn't need his professional opinion. That's what it was, after all. His professional side taking over, reminding him that people did desperate things all the time and almost always lived to regret it. Like when his uncle had insisted on taking a share of his aunt's money because he'd lost his job. Or when she'd refused to give even a penny because she'd already spent more than half on a closet full of absurd fur coats.

And then there was the realtor. Chase's eyes narrowed. He started his car and glanced at the upstairs window one last time. It was dark inside, leaving him to wonder if she was already asleep. He pulled away from the curb.

What had her conversation been with Mr. Craig that last moment before she'd gotten out of the car? He frowned into his rearview mirror and turned into his garage. The man had seemed... *interested*. Or maybe Chase was just reading into the one fear he kept locked deep down. If Abby was a patient of his, it would've been their first in-office conversation. Her constant searching for something better.

Chase had only slightly touched on the topic once before. Abby had been so upset by his mere suggestion that she struggled with appreciating what she had, that he hadn't dared to finish his explanation. His reasoning was because of growing up in such a broken home with so little love, she was constantly searching for her happily ever after, while at the same time fearing it completely. The moment she felt the slightest inkling that she may have found it, she would sabotage herself and start a search for something new.

CHAPTER 10

Chase stood at Abigail's door so long it felt like hours. He refused to apologize. After all, what had he done besides given his advice? *Good* advice. But when he heard a muffled sound from the other side of the door, it was nearly impossible to resist hurling it open again and begging for forgiveness.

He placed his hand on the wood, wishing things had gone very differently. When he'd come over that afternoon, he'd wanted to help her stay grounded. Maybe give her some direction. He thought for sure she would give up when he refused to help with repairs. But it hadn't swayed her.

She'd seemed so out of control before when she hinted about buying the Poppyridge house. To Chase, it had been a desperate act by someone who'd never had anything and had suddenly been given everything. And he had a long history of that. It all started when his Aunt Lynn had won the state lottery. A fairly small amount that managed to do a great deal of damage to their family.

"And fixing up a house is so much work." He shook his head. "I don't want any part of it. I'm sorry."

She felt choked, balancing on the edge of tears but forcing them away as quickly as they came. "I never asked for your help," she returned, wishing she couldn't see how much it hurt him. But these were her dreams she was talking about—trusting him with. And he'd seemed more supportive about her designing labels. "Goodnight."

He was still looking back at her when the door closed. She covered her mouth, trying to stop herself from crying. But her vision blurred, and a breath escaped in a sob. And then another. Her heart ached, and she leaned against the door wishing he would come back. She wanted his arms around her, familiar and kind. Always hopeful and adoring.

Why couldn't he support her on this? She wiped at her tear-stained cheeks, but the tears kept falling. Her heart kept breaking. Even as she dragged her feet to her bedroom and showered. Brushed her teeth. Climbed into bed.

It still hurt. And her eyes were raw from tears as if there were simply none left. She laid on her pillow and stared up at the ceiling for so long, it felt like the entire night should have passed. But eventually she drifted into sleep, only to dream of beheaded animals being gruesomely tossed into a pile.

deposited on the deck. The police officer could be wrong. Even though he realized it was highly unlikely, he made a mental list of animals that were capable of killing. His only thoughts were bear and wolves, both of which were unheard of in the area.

His next avenue of thought came more easily, being something he confronted every day. Human behavior. What would make someone act in such a way? They had to first have an end goal, like scaring buyers off or somehow hoping to prove themselves. Perhaps they wanted only to gain attention. But why?

Chase stacked the last storage bin atop another and tried to pick the single most likely scenario. It wasn't easy, but eventually, he decided that scaring buyers off was the option that made the most sense. And that turned his thoughts to Abigail.

She was the buyer, after all. His heart pinched as he imagined her walking around the house and beach with her realtor friend. And then coming back to find another animal. Chase's heart beat faster, thinking over what had to happen in that small window of time, and what the person might have looked like. Or more importantly, what kind of web his mind must have been twisted into.

Suddenly Chase straightened, imagining something new. A question came to his mind that he didn't know the answer to, and it felt more significant than anything else. Abigail's friend, the realtor... had they been separated at all during their time at the house? Perhaps it was enough time for him to kill the animal and stash it on the deck. And he would always know when new buyers were coming and going. Only with Abigail, that visit had been a last-minute decision. So, he wouldn't have had time until they were already there. Maybe he wanted to buy the house himself but needed more time. Or maybe he wanted it to go to auction, so he could bid on it. The more Chase thought it over, the more plausible it seemed.

He stood with a sudden energy and decided what he needed was a brisk walk. In hardly three minutes time, he headed out the door still wiping the dust from his hands.

When he ended up at Abigail's front steps, he paused a moment and looked up at her window, wondering what she was thinking of him. He'd managed to keep his thoughts well away from the topic all day. But now he'd stopped himself long enough to have a healthy kick of fear spread through his chest. She hadn't called or texted at all that day.

He pulled his phone from his pocket and tapped out a quick message.

Hello Bee, what are you up to? Can I come over?

He hesitated to push send, wondering just how mad she was... and if she would even reply.

"Chase!"

He spun around, nearly dropping his phone. Abigail was walking fast, closing the space between them with a smile stretched across her beautiful face. She was a dazzling sight, and it was a moment before Chase noticed she held a red leash in one hand and had an animal in tow.

He was so shocked he didn't even reply, only stared at the floppy-eared, clumsy bundle of energy padding alongside her.

Not that it was so incredibly surprising. Abigail loved

animals, after all. But her apartment had barely enough room for her. Adding an animal had always been out of the question. Or... so Chase had thought. If he'd had any idea she wanted one so badly, he would've researched and planned until he'd found just the right breed. But whatever Abigail had bumping along next to her, he doubted there'd been much research.

He finally woke from his immobile state to lift a hand in greeting, but she only laughed at him and held up a large, glittering envelope. Bright turquoise that shimmered like a tropical fish just pulled from the reef.

"I got my first letter!" She was out of breath, still reeling from whatever had possessed her to run out and purchase a puppy. Her cheeks were flushed with a healthy shade of pink, and her eyes were vibrant and alive. Chase admired her a moment longer, and a smile spread across his face.

"Here, read it," she persisted, nearly punching him in the jaw with the letter as she tripped on puppy feet. Her hand reached for him, and she steadied herself. "Oh—sorry."

She took a step back and seemed to suddenly remember the day before. Her eyes glanced across his, questioning and unsure. And the vibrancy in her features wavered.

He took the letter. "What's this?" he asked, wishing he'd shaken off the shock before her smile had fallen. For a moment, it was like the night before had never happened. But now it returned in her eyes, and he could feel an uncomfortable sensation in his middle. The painful reminder that something was unresolved.

"It's my first challenge, and I've already completed it." Her explanation dropped off into giggles as the gangly, rust-colored puppy jumped up. It pawed at her legs and licked her hand incessantly when she reached down, eager to prove its love. She laughed again and Chase opened the letter, scanning over it quickly.

It was hand-written, in the same beautiful scrawl as before. Aunt Sharalyn. There was hardly a paragraph, and it sounded more like a sonnet than actual communication. But the challenge was clear. Do the first spontaneous thing you can think of.

So that was it. The reason Abigail had decided to buy a puppy that couldn't possibly fit in her apartment. But she was glancing back at Chase now, looking enchantingly unsure of herself. Chase wanted nothing more at that moment than to wrap his arms around her, but he'd left on such bad terms the night before, he hardly knew what to say.

"That's great," he finally answered, handing the letter back. He meant to say more, or maybe bring up their disagreement. But as he looked back at her, he couldn't find the words. He couldn't bring himself to support her buying the Poppyridge house, and that's what it would take to end their dispute. But at least he could try to smooth things over.

"Thanks," she answered quietly.

They both glanced around at the air between them, and Chase finally took a tentative step. The puppy jumped up on his legs, mistaking his closeness for an invitation. He smiled. "About last night," he began, speaking carefully.

She shook her head, about to wave the conversation

away, but he caught her hand in his. "I'm just worried about you." He held her hand gently, and half expected her to pull away. But she didn't. "I can't agree with you on this. It just seems so sudden and... *reckless*, don't you think?" He hoped she would appear a little bit persuaded, but her features were set in firm determination.

"Maybe if you just waited until you've completed these challenges—it looks like it won't be anything too crazy." He smiled a bit, loving the way it always seemed to distract her. "No scaling buildings, at least for now."

Her lips edged upwards, and she glanced down at his feet. It looked like she was fighting to keep her smile from growing. "I'll think about it," she finally answered.

Chase exhaled quietly, still holding her hand in his. He couldn't help but notice how soft her skin was and how delicate her hand felt. So many little things about her delighted him.

Her puppy jumped up again, pulling him from his thoughts. He reached his hand out to pet the bundle of energy and slobber. "By the way…" He paused, trying to get the puppy to relax a bit. "Just where are you going to keep this guy?"

"I haven't come up with anything yet. I just saw a box of puppies for sale outside the community center and had to take a look, I'm sure I'll think of something." She shrugged it off like it wasn't a problem. The look on her face was pure, resolved happiness. She smiled at the puppy like it had brightened not only her day but her life.

Chase studied her face long enough to realize there was something more than just a fun, spontaneous decision going on with her. She'd somehow genuinely changed since the night before. Even if it was only a tiny shift in her thinking… it showed.

"You can keep him at my place," he offered, almost surprising himself. He'd decided in a fraction of a second, but there was no regret. If anything on this earth brought Abigail as much happiness as that puppy seemed to, he was in favor of it. He suppressed the retaliation in his mind, telling him there was something else that brought her happiness. A big something else.

"Really?" She stood, taking her attention off the puppy and looking back at him with a sincerity that made her rich brown eyes deepen. "Are you sure? I thought you didn't want any pets."

"Well, I didn't really," he confessed. "I'd feel bad being gone all day. But I could give you a key to my place."

His eyes flickered up, and for a moment, he felt like a fraud trying to weasel her into a commitment of some kind. Their relationship had always stayed firmly in the separate dwelling territory, and for Chase, it had more to do with his concerns about her getting tired of him and moving on. "Maybe just until you find somewhere permanent?"

She smiled cautiously. "That would really help, thanks."

They headed down the walk together, back the way Chase had come. His apartment was a short walk away, but there were some serious hills in between. Abigail's poor puppy wobbled along in between them until it started to fall behind. They noticed at the same time, turning together.

"Here." Chase scooped the puppy up, trying to

maneuver its skinny legs and big paws until he finally had a comfortable hold. "I think this little guy's had it."

"His name's Champ." Abigail smiled. "He's my champion."

Chase held her eyes for a moment and finally turned back to the puppy. Its scruffy head was drooped over his arm. "You tired, Champ?" he asked, rubbing his soft fur. "That's a great name."

With the puppy in his arms, they made it up the last hill and to Chase's apartment. But Abigail didn't stay like she normally did. She rushed off, claiming she needed to stock up on supplies for Champ.

It made sense, especially with how spontaneous a purchase the puppy was. But it also left Chase wondering more deeply just where their relationship was at. They'd managed a pleasant conversation, sure. But had something been set into place that could somehow change their future? Had he pushed too hard?

Chase couldn't help but fear he'd done more than just disagree the night before. What if he'd placed a wedge between them? It was the exact opposite of what he'd wanted. Usually, when Chase felt this strongly about something, Abigail would recognize it and agree. It was how they'd treated each other all along. Chase could respect when Abigail felt passionate about something, and she always respected him as well. So, why didn't she do that now? What was so tempting about this place that she couldn't leave it alone? What was luring her there?

With each question, Chase felt more lost. Was she seriously considering moving to Poppyridge Cove long-term? *Living there?* Could she be choosing this house over *him*? Was it the new, shiny thing he'd been fearing would come?

He tried to keep the realtor out of his thoughts, but it was nearly impossible. They'd spent an entire day together alone, just the two of them. Which left plenty of time to talk. Maybe he came with the house… and maybe Chase already knew what that meant for him.

He shook himself from his thoughts, perfectly aware he'd let them spiral too far out of control. It was something he excelled at, and it could be quite helpful when trying to get to the root of a problem. But when combined with doubt and a pinch of fear, it was a recipe for red herring.

He ran a hand over his weary head, watching the sleeping puppy next to him. It really was a sweet creature. Looked to be part Labrador, although its coloring was redder than any Lab he'd ever seen. Abigail had a sense about things like that. He had no doubt her puppy would be the most naturally obedient and intelligent animal possible.

He'd learned from experience to trust her instincts.

He gazed out the front window to the small, spindly tree in the front yard. Is that what he needed to do now? Trust her? A headache swelled at the back of his neck at the mere thought. When he'd seen that house in the forest, it was dark and decrepit, like its days in the sun were long over. If it were up to him, he'd bulldoze the place and build an entirely new structure.

Champ woke enough to flop himself around and end up with his small head resting on Chase's leg. His glossy, black eyes blinked up at him.

Chase leaned down, staring into the puppy's face.

"What do you think?" he asked. The black eyes closed again, and he was instantly asleep. "You're right," Chase continued in a whisper, "I may be worrying over nothing. Maybe things will settle if I just stop stirring the water, ya know?"

Champ's ears twitched, and his head lifted.

"Ah, you thirsty?" He went to find a bowl in the kitchen with big puppy paws padding around him in a sudden blizzard of energy.

CHAPTER 11

Abby had rushed off so quickly, she'd hardly said two words to Chase. It was starting to grate on her conscience. But she had no choice, his eyes were painfully easy to read. The love she saw in them was crushing her, leaving her second-guessing her decision to buy the house at Poppyridge Cove and wondering if he was right. He was a very sensible thinker. Usually, she would talk to him for hours about the ins and outs of her decision. In the end, it would leave her certain of her answer.

But this time…

"Your total comes to $226.32, ma'am,"

Abby shook off her thoughts and snatched her credit card from her wallet, musing that free puppies were more expensive than she'd imagined.

She lugged the oversized, overstuffed plastic bag in one hand and a dog crate in the other, carrying them through the parking lot. Nearly out of breath, she managed to push the right button on her keys and pop the trunk of her car. She pushed her hip against the crate, only to have it catch the edge of the car frame and slide off. It clunked to the ground, jarring her shoulder. With a frustrated mumble, she tried again, this time making sure to throw the bag in first.

"Need some help?"

She recognized Vance's voice immediately, and her already swirling emotions seemed to combust in her chest.

He took the crate and positioned it just right in her car, and then he just stood there staring back at her. Looking into his eyes suddenly felt too intimate—too inviting. She swung her gaze back to her grocery bag instead, arranging the items that had tumbled out. She tied the handle pieces together and finally backed away, allowing him to close the trunk.

"Thanks," she said, fidgeting with her jeans and not sure what to do with her hands. She rested them on her hips, but a mental picture of Wonder Woman sprang to her thoughts. She let them drop, hanging at her sides.

"You're welcome," he said with a smile, grinning through the words. "So, did you get a pet?"

"I did. A puppy." She wanted to get into her car before he could misread her nerves again. But mostly she thought about how he'd held her hand, and she hadn't pulled away. She swallowed, wishing she would have.

"Oh, nice," he nodded through the silence, glancing around them as if admiring the day. "You know, I was thinking." He took a step closer. "If you wanted to get some paperwork completed now, we could have everything ready by next week when you do your final inspection of the Poppyridge place." He smiled again, holding her gaze firmly in his. "It might make things go more smoothly."

Abby felt trapped in his stare, and her throat was becoming dry. "That—" her voice caught, and she cleared her throat, "might be nice. Okay, let's plan on it." She nodded decisively, wanting to speed things along.

"Great," Vance nodded, but as he prepared to leave, he rested his hand on her arm.

She suddenly wished she'd worn long sleeves so she couldn't feel his fingers brush across her bare skin. He seemed to stand there forever, making her cheeks turn hot. "I'll give you a call tomorrow when I'm in the office."

"Okay, thanks," she mumbled, trying desperately to look bored. But as he walked away, she leaned back on her car weakly. Her hands shook, and she doubted she'd fooled him in the least. She couldn't keep skirting around what he was trying to do. He had to know she wasn't okay with it. She needed to tell him the very next time she spoke to him.

She pulled the door open and drove out of the parking lot with the strange feeling that he was watching. She checked her rearview mirror, just to be sure.

* * *

THE SKY WAS GETTING dark when she pulled up to Chase's apartment. Her hands had finally stilled, and she was becoming increasingly angry at herself for not speaking up with Vance. It almost seemed like he knew her trigger points and just how hard to push so that she wouldn't react. She hoped she was wrong about him, but she didn't want to be taken advantage of, either. If there was one thing her rotten childhood had done, it'd been to give her a healthy suspicion of anyone and everyone.

She stomped up the pretty, stained concrete steps. They were flourished with a cobblestone design, although too glossy and seamless to be authentic. She'd managed to wrangle the crate and overstuffed grocery bag again, and this time she didn't want anyone's help. She pushed the doorbell with her toe, hopping on one leg.

Chase opened the door, and a look of surprise crossed his face. "Whoa, hey I can get that for you,"

"No," she said shortly, wedging herself and all the supplies through the door together. The toe of her shoe caught on the entrance and she tripped forward, setting everything down in a half-fall.

Chase stared back at her, still holding the door open and looking either irritated or confused… or both. She couldn't tell. "Thanks though," she finished, hoping to appear normal. But she didn't *feel* normal. She felt taken advantage of. Intimidated. It had her going over her conversation with Vance again and again, only to hash out the perfect phrase of words that could have put him in his place.

"Well"—Chase stepped over the large grocery bag—"Champ slept the whole time. I took him out once to kill a nice spot of grass in the backyard, and besides that, he's just been a big couch potato."

Abby walked across the room quietly and sat down next to Champ—*her puppy*. She still couldn't believe it. It made her feel five years old again and stirred up a bubbling excitement from somewhere deep inside. A place where reality and dreams blurred into a singular thought and everything was beautiful.

She ran her hand along his back, rubbing his silky puppy coat. His eyes squeezed together in a sleeping blink, but he didn't wake. "Thanks for taking care of him," she said, without looking up.

"You're welcome, Abigail."

Her gaze lifted at his tone. The way he'd said her name felt more like a confession of his feelings than mere conversation.

He crossed the room to sit down next to her. His fragrance was amazing, like sandalwood… and something else she couldn't pinpoint. It nearly had her eyes closing in the comfort of his presence.

But she reminded herself that she was still irritated with him. Why he was so dead set on her staying in her dingy apartment with her boring job? Why couldn't he let her dream bigger than that? She eyed him thoughtfully. It seemed to be the cue he was waiting for.

He reached for her hand. "I need to explain myself, I think," he began, glancing up at her. "There are reasons why I'm not encouraging you to go ahead and buy the house."

Abby lifted her eyebrow, and he paused.

"Okay, okay, I'm completely against you buying the house." He smiled a bit. "You know about my Aunt Lynn, right?"

Abby worked hard not to roll her eyes. "Chase, this is nothing like her situation, and I am nothing like Aunt Lynn." She'd pulled her hand from his and tossed it into the air as she spoke. "Fur coats are completely different from buying a home. And this isn't just any house,

Chase. This could be an incredible opportunity for—me."

She'd hesitated on that last word, wanting to say *us* so badly, but he wasn't partnering with her on this. "Using my degree in design to bring this amazing piece of history back to life, and creating a space for people to come stay, and enjoy not only an inn on the coast but a private strip of sand beyond that, and a protected redwood forest in the backyard." She stopped, marveling at the thought again and wondering how it had even become possible for her.

Her.

Abigail Tanner. Growing up nearly an orphan and going from designing product labels to *this*. It was a dream come true. She was lost in her thoughts when he shifted his position, facing her.

"I know that sounds amazing. But you're leaving a lot out. What about the condition of the house? It's falling apart."

"Not on the inside—" she insisted.

"I guarantee you, it's going to need so much work. The plumbing, the electricity. Things are going on below the surface—there always are!" He shook his head. "But that would be expected in a house like this. What isn't expected is the strange occurrences there."

Abby couldn't help but groan. It was strange, yes. But she had no doubt it would stop, eventually. Someone was just messing around.

"Abigail, it's serious. It scares me. It's demented. What on earth could explain it? And why would you walk into a purchase when you have no idea if your life would be in danger because of it?"

A tingle of fear trickled up Abby's spine, and she looked back soberly, considering Chase's words.

"I don't know why you aren't satisfied with the thought of a normal, productive life. You have a great job and live in a nice area, but it never seems like enough. I know you don't want to hear this, but I'm worried that you're fighting a few demons from your past. You might not be aware of it manifesting itself in this huge, sudden decision."

"Stop." Abby held her hand up, feeling almost out of control. She tightened her inner grip on her emotions. "It was rough, that's for sure. And I've trusted you enough to share my past with you. But it's in the past. It's finished with. Done. I don't need you bringing it up every time we disagree about something."

Her voice trembled, and she could feel her heart picking up its pace. She was losing her grip, but this was important. She needed to say it. She wasn't going to be intimidated into staying silent. Not again. "Why are you so afraid to dream of more, Chase? You're content to sit in your pretty house and work at your ordinary job and that's it! Don't you want more?"

She looked back at his face, and her heart sunk. He appeared more shocked than she'd realized, his mouth slack and nearly hanging open. It was an expression of someone who felt completely betrayed, and she'd never meant to cause that.

"I just mean…" She wasn't sure how to finish. She'd said exactly what she meant.

Chase stood, resting his hands on his hips with his back to her. "Well, maybe we just aren't going in the same direction anymore."

The silence that followed was excruciating, with the one sentence he'd uttered digging a trench in her heart. He wasn't really breaking up with her over a house... was he?

"I'm happy to watch Champ, but I think we should take some time to figure out what we both want." His voice had changed. It was firm. Threatening, like a final ultimatum.

And she wasn't going to stand for it.

Abby pushed off the couch and brushed past him. "I know what I want." She pulled the door open and left without another glance.

Her chest burned as she walked down the steps with the fear of what had just happened. She'd been with Chase for so long, and they'd hardly ever argued—and never seriously. Now she has this amazing opportunity, and he ditches her, just like that?

Her vision blurred as she started her car, and the burning in her chest expanded to her throat, sizzling hot like she was going to ignite. She cranked the radio up, hoping to drown out her thoughts as she sped back to her house. Her apartment. Is that where he wanted her to stay? Is that where he thought she belonged?

Her tears couldn't be restrained any longer, and they streamed down her cheeks as she rushed upstairs to her door. The musty, unkept odor of her apartment seemed more invasive than usual, inviting her in obnoxiously. Like it was a vindictive relative bent on keeping her down. She'd known enough of those, and quietly in her mind, she thanked the heavens that they'd all left this earth long before. No one was around to hold her back or weasel her portions away.

Suddenly she was eight years old again, holding a beautiful locket given to her as a birthday present by a caring teacher. A teacher who probably knew a little about her home life. It was stainless steel and more expensive than anything in her entire house. She'd been in awe of how it shined and reflected images, like a gem in her smudged-mirror life.

And of course, her mother noticed right away. She'd had to tell Mrs. Rainwater that she didn't wear it to school because she didn't want to risk losing it, instead of the truth. That her mother had stolen it and likely sold it to pay for her addictions. She'd never seen that locket again.

But this time her mother wasn't around to suck the hope from her life.

If she wanted to design the most incredible seaside inn the world had ever seen, she was going to do it. And nothing would get in her way. No one would dissuade her. If they tried, she'd walk away, like she should have done when she was little. But now she thanked her mom. Strangely, losing that locket had given her hands the strength to hold on to even larger dreams. Dreams she wasn't going to let anyone take away.

She fell asleep trying not to think of Chase or everything he'd done for her over the years. The way he'd supported her through college, always available to study through the night for a test. Or bring her lunch at work because he knew she was picking up an extra shift. His smile made its way into her thoughts too. The way it caught her off guard that first day they'd met. His athletic build combined with his smile was almost overwhelming. She'd never understood just what he saw in her, but she hadn't wanted to push her luck by asking. If for some reason, he'd believed he wanted her above anyone else, she had just wanted to go with it.

But it seemed the magic had worn off. Maybe he'd finally peered through her rebuilt image and right down to the damaged little girl underneath.

Abby's tears returned, trailing onto her pillow.

CHAPTER 12

The office was very modern. And clean. Even the handles on the tall glass doors gleamed with her reflection. Abby had every intention of holding her own this time. As she walked down the hallway and arrived at Vance's door, she reviewed a dozen phrases she'd thought up beforehand. Just in case he found a way to turn her into a bundle of nerves again.

She hesitated in the open doorway, glancing back at the empty desk where his secretary usually sat.

"Come in," his voice called from inside the office. He sounded pleasant enough. Abby walked through, taking a seat and waiting for him to look up from his computer screen. "Okay." He still stared at the screen, finally turning to her. "I've printed off everything we need, but my secretary had to run home with a sick child, so let me just go get those, and we can begin."

"Great," Abby said as he brushed past, whisking down the hall quickly. He didn't seem at all interested in her as more than a client. Relief flooded through Abby, and she relaxed more fully into her seat.

"So these"—Vance appeared with a large stack of papers—"should be all you need. Don't worry about the number of pages, you'll only have to sign a few." He nodded at her briefly and then went back to organizing the stack of pages he held. After separating the bundle into half a dozen piles, he lifted the first.

"Here we go."

He detailed each page neatly and clearly, and Abby found herself impressed with the way he was able to explain it all so fully. The stack of pages took them less than an hour to complete, with him asking her questions and ensuring she understood every detail. He was very good at what he did. She'd almost forgotten about her nerves from the day before. Still, she didn't like the feeling he gave her, as if he knew how to elicit the reactions he wanted. It was just a feeling, but she made sure to remind herself who was working for who.

"And that's it." He stacked the papers together and tucked them into a folder. "The only thing left to do is decide on a time to inspect the property." He lifted his eyebrows and waited.

"Oh." Abby quickly reviewed her week while trying not to notice how much free time she had if she wasn't going to be spending it with Chase. "I can do anytime. How about tomorrow?"

"Tomorrow?" Vance sat back a little in his chair, "Well, okay, if you think you're ready to decide by then."

Again, he paused with his eyebrows raised. His eyes weren't imploring her the way they had before, just blandly gazing like she was a poster on the wall. Maybe that was the way he liked to behave at work. Professional and distant. And if so, she was glad. She'd had enough of his sly advances.

"I will," she said confidently, although her insides swirled with indecision. If only she could talk to Chase about it, but he'd already made his decision.

Vance gave her nothing more than a curt goodbye, and she breathed a sigh of relief on the way out.

She pictured the house as she drove away. The interior had been breathtaking, with classic indulgences that newer homes just didn't have. From the heavy, carved railing on the stairs, to the elegant ballroom with its embellished floors, walls, and ceilings. It was incredible. She'd never expected anything like that. It wouldn't need half the work inside that she'd thought.

But the outside... She cringed. It was bad. And there wasn't much she knew about remodeling the exterior of buildings. The bones. She knew all about designing the space within, but it was Chase who had all the experience in building.

He'd worked in construction through college for a renowned builder. It was the perfect work experience for a job like this.

She pulled up to his apartment and dug in her purse for the key he'd given her, thankful it was early enough in the afternoon that he'd still be at work, though it hurt just thinking about him like that. She unlocked the door and walked in quietly, listening to the silence for a moment.

"Champ?" she called, wandering into the living room. The dog bed she'd bought had been placed by the back sliding door, where he could look out at the backyard. Champ was snuggled up on it, but his head popped up. At the sight of her, he jumped up and scrambled over. His ears flapped against the side of his head, and Abby laughed, bending down to pet him.

Chase walked out from the hall with steam still rising from his skin. Abby gasped, nearly falling over. He had a towel wrapped around his waist and was rubbing his head with another one, covering his face. But the instant he dropped it, their eyes met.

He froze, leaning to one side as if slightly off-balance. "Oh." He lowered the towel from his head, exposing his built chest.

Abby didn't remember him looking quite as magazine-like the last time she'd seen him with his shirt off. It'd been at a pool party a few weeks back, but clearly he'd been working out.

"I didn't realize you were here," he continued, rolling the hand towel into a ball and causing his arms to bulge impressively. Abby tried not to notice.

"Yeah, sorry, I thought you were at work." She shifted her weight from foot to foot, feeling more devastated by the second. If he were any closer, she couldn't have resisted stepping into his arms. And his favorite fragrance was stronger than ever—he smelled amazing.

"I took the day off," he said. His voice sounded sad. Abby studied his face and the way he gazed back at her. What was he not saying?

But silence prevailed, and he didn't explain.

"Well, I'll just take Champ for a walk then." Abby lifted the leash from a hook on the wall and clipped it onto the puppy's collar. Chase hadn't moved. He just looked back at her with his lips pulled downward. "I'll see ya."

But she didn't see him. When she returned from her walk, the house was empty. She even made a point of checking his bedroom. Again, she wished they could talk. Maybe he was right. Maybe they were just headed in different directions, and it wouldn't work. A lump formed in her throat, and she took a deep breath, encouraging it away.

As soon as she had a space for Champ, she'd take him with her. That, or she'd feel this rotten pain every day. She wiped her eyes and left, wishing Chase well in her heart.

* * *

HER DRIVE to the house with Vance had been quick, with Abby's excitement and apprehension battling it out on her insides until she felt nearly strangled. When they arrived, all she could think of was the back porch. She looked at Vance as they got out of his car, and his eyes were already gazing at her. He tilted his head toward the house and she nodded.

It was a beautiful day, with the sun shining hot and strong around them. Abby inched closer to Vance as they neared the back corner of the house, but when they stepped around to see the porch in view, it was clear.

Abby exhaled and Vance smiled. "Looks like you might be in luck," he said. "Maybe this animal hater finally got the point. I requested a patrol car to check up on the area every few days or so—might've helped."

"Oh." Abby looked back at him, appreciating his extra effort and thought. "Thank you."

He nodded back, polite and distant. There wasn't anything about his behavior that made her uncomfortable. She wondered if she'd simply read too much into his mannerisms before. "I think we should still set up the camera though," she added.

"Definitely." He returned to the car and came back with it in his hands. Glancing up at the building, his eyes were narrowed in thought. "Where do you think would be best?"

Abby studied the house with him and finally decided on a corner nook that looked like it would provide enough cover for the device not to be seen. "How about there—up in that corner?"

"Perfect." Vance turned to her, watching her face for a moment. "This is your day to make a final decision, Abby. Why don't you walk through the property and building for as long as you need while I work on securing the camera?"

With a deep breath, Abby nodded. Chills traveled down her arms and tingled on her fingertips at the thought of owning the house. It seemed to call to her heart, and she was listening intently. But she also wanted to be sure. *Absolutely* sure. She stilled her excitement and walked around the back of the house, admiring the full view of the sea in the day's ample sunlight. It sparkled clear to the horizon.

This time, she wanted to enter the house from the front. It was neglected and almost in shambles, but she could imagine a grand entrance. With the fountain in front gleaming serenely and stone pathways winding about, it wouldn't be too complicated to transform the property.

She walked inside to a large open entrance that looked out onto the luxurious staircase. It was immediately clear what was missing. If she was to have an ocean view, she wanted it everywhere. She drew up a mental picture of the space with a double set of windows showing off the ocean sunsets. She couldn't imagine anything more perfect. The aged surroundings would be incredible when paired with new, modern touches. She walked through every room, taking her time upstairs and marveling at the view of the cove from the largest corner bedroom. A small curl of sand was visible behind the hill with the waves crashing against it.

"What do you think?"

Abby spun around to find Vance standing in the doorway. He was lit from behind, with shadows on his face that made it hard to see his expression. A pinch of discomfort twisted in her stomach, but she kept her chin up and shoulders squared. "I love it," she announced. "Just as much as I have every time before."

"So you've decided? You're one hundred percent in?"

She nodded with a confident smile on her lips. There was no question.

He lifted his cell phone in one hand. "Want me to make the call?"

She listened as he made the official-sounding agreement and was surprised at how quickly he hung up the phone. A life's decision summed up in a mere handful of sentences. It was disorienting.

"Well, Abby…" Vance walked slowly closer until he was standing by her side. "Welcome home."

A grin spread across her face. It was like a dream. "Thank you, I can hardly believe it." She wandered back through the room cautiously and down the staircase, trailing one hand along the smoothly carved railing, appreciating its strength and history all the more, and wondering who had walked those steps before her. How long had such a beautiful piece of history stood vacant? She felt a sacred responsibility settle in her heart as if she'd rescued a priceless treasure from near destruction.

When she came to the back door she paused, hesitating. Vance's footsteps on the staircase were heavy and slow as if he was watching her. But she still waited, remembering the scene on the porch and the images from her dream. With a quick breath, she pulled the door open and stepped outside… onto an empty deck.

Her hand settled on her chest lightly, calming her heart. The trail camera was barely visible in the corner nook, tucked away expertly.

"Should give us a pretty good shot of anyone coming onto the porch," Vance said quietly, standing behind her. The deep strength in his voice suddenly felt reassuring. She'd gradually begun to trust him throughout the day. "And you know, I've been thinking,"

Vance stepped around her, touching her back as he passed by. "If you need some help managing repairs and things like that, I'd be happy to come out." He shrugged. "I don't have a huge load of clients at the moment, and this place is pretty amazing. It'd be my pleasure." His eyes gazed steadily into hers, waiting.

Abby looked across the surroundings, wondering where she would start. The grounds needed quite a bit of help as well. And the more she inspected, the more she began to notice just what a crumbling state the exterior of the house had become. She quickly began to feel overwhelmed.

If only Chase could—she stopped herself in the thought. She was going this alone. And if Vance was more than happy to help, why wouldn't she accept his offer? He'd been perfectly respectful all day, leaving her to wonder if she hadn't just let her nerves get the better of her.

"Okay," she finally answered, turning to him with a curt nod. Any other person, she would have given into her excitement and nearly hugged the life out of them. But not Vance. She still felt cautious, like he might be keeping something from her. But she couldn't afford to pass up a willing volunteer.

They returned to his car, and she watched the house as they backed away, admiring its position in the surrounding wilderness. It only got better with each new angle. When they started down the road, she noticed the older gentleman they'd seen before was out in front of his house cleaning up leaves—Mr. Fillmore, if she remembered the neighbor's conversation correctly.

"Do you mind if we stop and chat for a minute?" she asked. Getting to know the neighbors was something she'd been anticipating. The thought of becoming part of their small, beautiful community was a thrill.

Vance glanced at the clock and pulled to the side of the road. "Sure, I've got time for a quick hello."

Mr. Fillmore turned at the sound of their car doors closing, and a smile creased his kind, wrinkled face. "Well, hello there," he called, "not having car trouble, are you?" He set down his hedge clippers and met them halfway across the perfect, green grass. Abby admired the tidy appearance of his landscaping. "No, no." She held a hand out. "I just wanted to introduce myself since we're going to be neighbors soon."

His eyebrows lifted, crinkling his forehead in a delighted show of surprise. "Oh yeah? You buying the Poppyridge house then?" He shook her hand, reaching for Vance's next. "Well you two have got your work cut out for you, that's for sure. Good thing you're young and healthy." He chuckled, although Abby cut in as quickly as she could.

"Oh no, this is my realtor, Vance. I'm buying the house. My name's Abby."

His face had fallen at her explanation, with his eyes narrowing in a disapproving look. "You? Just you?"

Abby nodded.

"Well, I mean no disrespect, but you do know there are… strange things going on up there from time to time? I'd worry about a cute little gal like you being all alone out here."

"No need to worry," she assured, ignoring the chills at the back of her neck. "I won't be alone. I'll be hiring out the labor and working with quite a few professionals on this project. I'm sure by the time we're finished, we'll be able to clear the area of anything suspicious."

"Ah, okay," he agreed, still with a look of concern on his face. "It's nice to meet you, Abby. Don't hesitate to ask for help if you need anything. I'm retired and, most of the time, *bored*." He laughed again before shaking their hands a second time and returning to his hedge.

It felt good meeting the members of her little community, although Abby wished he wouldn't have made a big deal of the *suspicious happenings* at her house. She was beginning to wonder if everyone on the street would react the same way, and if they did, were they right? Was her dream house really a terrible risk? It didn't feel like a risk to her, it just felt right. She'd never felt better about a decision in her life. For once, she had the perfect plan and the means to complete it.

Maybe her dreams really were coming true.

CHAPTER 13

Securing a construction team had been a headache, but worth it. Abby loved researching past projects and fighting for her spot with the best team she could find. But it didn't come cheap. She pushed the numbers to the back of her mind, assuring herself that the money would be there in no time. Once she completed all her challenges, everything would be settled. The first challenge had been a breeze, after all. She'd fallen in love with Champ and wondered why it'd taken her so long to get a dog.

She pulled up to Chase's apartment and a dozen memories hit her all at once. Memories of movie nights and bowls of ice cream snuggled up on his couch. Times when he'd secretly taken work off just to help her with something he knew she was stressing about. He was the best relationship she'd ever had... and it had withered away without even a struggle.

To her, it seemed he'd just given up. The second they disagreed on something, while admittedly a huge something, he just called it quits. But then, she hadn't put up much of a fight to keep him there. Deep down, she'd always known it wouldn't last. Something so good just wasn't real, except when it came to the house at Poppyridge. *That* was a dream come true, one that wouldn't fade away.

She blew her hair from her face with a sigh and walked up the steps. Champ spotted her from behind the window curtain and barked, except he seemed to know he wasn't allowed to bark, and the resulting inner puppy conflict created a half-choked squeak.

Abby pushed the door open and pointed to the floor. "Down," she warned, edging in before he could run outside and greet the world with his abundant friendliness. Champ's rump plopped down in front of her for half a second before he was on his feet again. "Good boy." She rubbed his head and tossed a miniature tennis ball across the room, sending him barreling away.

Another sigh escaped her, and she felt suddenly exhausted. Champ had a way of glomming onto any surrounding energy and stealing it away. Or maybe she'd just been taking too few breaks. She'd been known to work too hard for too long and make herself sick. Champ had retreated to his bed, chewing on his foot and the ball at the same time.

Abby smiled, but it wavered as she gazed across the apartment. There were still signs of her, from her umbrella propped by the door, to the cozy flannel throw draped across the couch. It had been Chase's birthday present from her. She trailed one hand along the back of a leather chair, remembering a particularly amazing kiss from a few months back. She glanced behind her cautiously before sneaking down the hall and peering into his bedroom. The curtains were still drawn, only letting a small bit of light in around the edges.

She continued to the dresser where a picture frame sat. It held a new picture of them together, one she hadn't seen in a long time. She wondered if he'd recently set it out. Her mind was instantly submerged in the memory of the summer they'd first met. He'd taken her to the fair. When they'd eaten too much cotton candy, they'd both nearly become sick, and everything seemed so funny they could hardly stop laughing.

Her heart throbbed painfully with a feeling of loss. Even if they were still friends, kind and awkwardly polite, it was crushing to think of him ever being with anyone else. She lifted the frame and studied their carefree faces until she heard the sound of the front door opening.

It jolted her from her thoughts, and she brushed at her wet eyes, replacing the frame to its place with a quick swipe of her hand. But it tottered on the edge of the dresser. She reached for it, only to bump it with her fingertips and send it crashing to the floor. "Oh no," she muttered, hurrying to pick up the pieces.

She could hear Chase behind her, his feet shuffling to a stop. What was he doing home, anyway? He was supposed to be at work. Her cheeks were burning hot, and she tried to blink away the tears in her eyes before they could trail down her face.

But he didn't say a word, and only lowered, picking up the frame along with a few pieces of glass and returning it to its place. "Did you cut yourself?" he finally asked, his voice sounding quiet in the enclosed bedroom. He reached for her hand, but she stood quickly.

A tear trailed down her cheek, and she brushed it away before he could see. "I'm fine," she rushed. "I'm sorry, I didn't mean to break it." Her voice had crumbled into a sob, and she dropped her face into one hand, trying to wrestle the emotions away. It was too hard to even look into his eyes, and she wasn't sure she wanted to see his reaction, anyway. He probably thought she was completely pathetic.

She sniffed back the tears and brushed at her shirt, straightening the fabric. "I didn't know you'd be home." She kept her eyes at his chest, refusing to look up. "I'd better go," she said, hurrying past him and into the hall.

"Wait, Abby," he said. His voice was quiet, leaving her to wonder if he even wanted to talk to her. Maybe he wished she would just leave. He followed her to the door, then simply stood looking back at her as he shifted his weight from one foot to the next.

Abby finally lifted her eyes to his and was sure she'd been right. His cheeks were flushed, and he looked very nearly angry. She swallowed.

"I'm sorry I surprised you," he began before taking a breath and blowing it out. Abby wondered if he was trying to control his anger. "I've changed my work schedule up, so it's a little sporadic now." Again, he shifted his weight. "Maybe if we had a set time for you to come over—no, never mind." He shook his head. "You can come see Champ whenever you want. He's your dog."

"I can take him with me in a week or so," Abby managed, clearing her throat and forcing her memories down deep. "I'll be staying up at the construction site until it's complete, keeping an eye on things. Champ will love it out there."

Chase didn't respond, and she hoped he wasn't making a mental countdown of the days. She could see a few scratch marks on various corners around his house. Maybe Champ had been more of an imposition than she'd thought.

"Or maybe I could just take him now if you want," she offered. "He's probably ruining your furniture."

"No," he cut in, slapping his hand on his leg and whistling. Champ came bounding over, forgetting about the tennis ball and slobbering all over Chase instead. He laughed and rubbed the puppy's floppy ears. "I'll miss him as it is. I don't mind."

"Oh." Abby felt a little ridiculous as her own puppy paid her absolutely no attention. "I'm glad he hasn't been too much of a pain."

"Not at all," Chase assured, gazing back at her as a few awkward minutes passed

"I'll see you later," she managed, fleeing out his door, only to drive away feeling like a fool. He was fine without her. Maybe he worried that she was a basket case, but he seemed to be doing great for himself. At least, he'd never looked more fit. And he was genuinely happy with a dog, which he swore he never wanted. So maybe it was all for the best then. But if it was, why was her chest throbbing like it'd been pierced clean through?

When she made it to her apartment, she caught sight of a bright gold envelope in her mailbox. An oversized one just like before. "Oh good," she sighed, pulling it from the old metal box and tearing it open as she stepped inside. She couldn't wait to have her mind on something other than Chase. But as she read the small poetic paragraph, she wondered just what her mystical aunt was trying to accomplish.

The message was simple enough. She was to go out for a day, choosing activities that she loved, and spoil herself. And she wasn't allowed to think of anyone else, just her. It was a challenge to be completely selfish for one day. Abby smiled, wishing she could have a chat with Sharalyn. She'd ask her what the point was of these challenges, and when she'd taken the time to create them. Had she scribbled them out quickly or were they the result of a great deal of thought?

Abby doubted that. They seemed to be so whimsical that they were nearly pointless. But if Abby was being forced to spoil herself for a day, she knew just how to do it.

* * *

Her wetsuit kept her warm enough to feel truly relaxed, even if the bay water was always frigid. The temperature outside hovered in the high 80s, making for a glorious day on the water. Her paddleboard had been stored in the garage for far too long as it was, and it felt good to have a breeze ruffling through her curls. The water was smooth and deep, always communicating with her, like a living creature, the way it moved and swelled in a constant state of change.

Her day had started with breakfast at a little café she'd always loved, in a quaint part of town with a beautiful view of the Bay Bridge. But the portions were so small she'd never gone there with Chase. She was sure he'd have to order a few breakfasts at least to fill up. But now that she'd enjoyed such a wonderful start to her day, she thought maybe he'd like it after all. Why hadn't she ever asked?

The water rippled to one side, sending a small wave passing by. She was panicked only for a moment before a dolphin's dorsal fin appeared, and then she relaxed again, watching the creature tilt its head to investigate. Its dark eye seemed unusually intelligent, and she held her hand out, skimming the water between them. It's long bottlenose tipped up quickly, tapping her palm before diving down again. The glossy curve of its body followed before sinking deep with a swish of its strong tail.

Abby laid back on her board and closed her eyes as the sun's rays slowly sank through her wetsuit. Her mind quieted with only of the sound of water interrupted by rocks and the distant sloshing of waves against the shore. The breeze could be heard ruffling through trees somewhere up in the hills. Cars beyond that, and the noise of the city.

She let her perspective shallow and enjoyed the way the water slapped her board and grazed her toes. It filled her with an inner peace that strengthened her core clear to her bones. A commitment to visit the ocean regularly echoed in her mind, like the calls of a lonely relative. It had always been part of her, but for some reason, she'd let life pull her away. She resolved to make time for the things that filled her with this feeling—the euphoric bliss of being truly content. Plus, she couldn't have picked a better day for it. With her remodeling crew scheduled to begin in two days, she needed this moment of self-care.

Her board dipped and something brushed her hand. Jolting upright, she held on to the sides as it rocked in the wake of a ski boat. She'd drifted farther away from shore than she wanted, and the seaweed was getting thick.

She dipped her paddle in and pushed at the tangled strands, working to free herself from the patch of green so she could return to shore. But it was hard work. She pulled her legs from the water and tried again, digging her paddle in. Finally, her board slid over the network of bulbs and strands, and she kept her arms moving, plowing through it slowly.

A tiny dark creature appeared to her side, lifting its head from the water. Its fur was ruffled and scraggly, but its dark eyes and small nose were adorable. A sea otter with no fear. It paddled forward and held on to her oar, sniffing it and nibbling for a second before flipping back into the water. Abby waited and paid close attention to the ripples, picking out three more otters. They were right next to her, and she hadn't even noticed. She made sure to paddle more carefully until she was free of the seaweed and finally skimming back to shore.

Challenge two... complete.

The sun was already beginning to lose its strength, and she knew how to fill the last few hours of the day. She sent a text message to Emily, hoping she'd be free at the last minute to go to dinner.

Yes!! I'd love to!!! Emily replied with more exclamation points than was necessary, but it definitely got her point across.

Abby smiled, admiring the way her friend was so abundant with her feelings. Either it was all exuberance and joy or a lightning-and-thunder kind of day, where it was wisest for anyone nearby to seek refuge elsewhere. She was glad today wasn't a stormy one for her friend.

Emily's unimpressed face. "You remember me mentioning my long-lost Aunt Sharalyn?"

"Yes!" Emily's eyes glittered with excitement. "Oh my gosh, what did she want with you? Did you fly to England? I just can't even believe this."

"I did." Abby laughed. "It was amazing." She couldn't help thinking back to Chase and his help on her trip. He was always so sensible and intelligent. She missed having his opinion around to calm her craziness. "I'm sorry I was so mysterious before. I wasn't quite sure what was going on myself. But she really does have an inheritance for me. The only catch is, I need to earn it by completing these challenges she created."

"Oooh, how mysterious," Emily crooned.

Abby shrugged, "Well, yeah. Only, so far, it's been strange. It seems too easy, like she just had an idea one day and scribbled down these challenges. At first, I thought they were going to be hard."

The waiter arrived, and they both ordered. But the moment he left their table, Emily clasped her hands together. "I know what she's doing," she whispered, glancing around at the other tables. "She's stringing you along, letting you think you've got this in the bag. And then *wham!*" She slapped her hand on the table. "She asks you to donate an organ. Secretly she's still alive, and you're the only match." Her eyes were glowing with intrigue, and Abby burst out laughing.

"Oh my gosh, you're right! How did I not realize this? It must be a kidney."

"Must be." Emily winked, grinning her wicked "gotcha" smile.

But for a moment there, she'd had Abby nervous.

What if Emily was right, and there was some trick coming? Sharalyn didn't seem the type to do that, from the small bits of information Abby knew about her. But the feeling wouldn't leave her stomach. All through dinner, she couldn't dismiss the possibility that something big was coming. Something she wasn't ready for.

CHAPTER 14

Chase watched out the window as Abby drove away. She'd run from the apartment like it was on fire, but he couldn't nail down *why*. When he'd first seen her in his bedroom, it had been a strike of lightning directly to his heart. Plus, she was looking at the picture he loved more than anything... or cleaning up the pieces on the floor. It was a strange similarity to their relationship.

He'd wanted to reach out and touch her soft hair. Hold her delicate frame in his arms. But she'd already made her choice. A choice that had seemed to cost her hardly any effort. It had shaken him more than he would ever let her know, even if he'd been waiting for it to happen. He'd assumed it would be that realtor friend of hers, Vance. But the fact that she left him for a house was somehow more crushing. And she hadn't looked back. He always feared it would ruin them, her propensity to escape a happily ever after in an oblivious, self-sabotaging kind of way.

Champ bounded across the room and sniffed at his

legs, waking him from his vigil at the window. He patted the soft head and floppy ears and walked down the hall, into his bedroom. The curtains were drawn, making the light dim and almost as soft as her skin. He swallowed and pulled open his dresser drawer. She'd been standing right next to it. A small velvet box he'd nearly paid off.

He lifted the tiny lid and touched the delicate, glittering ring inside. The white gold was brilliant and pale with a deep diamond set in, scattering facets of light in a gorgeous display. It was set on a band more slender and graceful than any ring he'd ever seen, which was appropriate for a delicate beauty like Abby's.

She'd had tears in her eyes.

She'd tried to brush it away, but the light reflected off the wetness on her cheeks. What did that mean? His heart had nearly exploded in his chest as he'd stood there wondering, wanting so badly to tell her how he felt, but knowing that she already made her decision. And then, instead of explaining himself and perhaps making her feel welcome so she might stay, he'd stood there silently, likely driving her off.

He snapped the ring box shut and tossed it in the drawer, slamming it closed. He'd thought of selling the ring or returning it. But he couldn't, not when she was still part of his life. And that was only due to Champ, which was why he couldn't let the little dog go with her. Sure, his apartment had been scratched up a fair amount, but everything about the puppy reminded him of Abigail. His intelligence was astounding for one, and he was so loving and cheerful.

But soon he would lose both of them, and he had to be ready for that. He had to steel his nerves and quit hiding everything away at the gym. He nearly lived there now. Work, gym, eat, sleep... repeat. It was barely enough distraction to keep him from thinking about her every second of the day. Now she only tortured his thoughts when he slept, visiting every dream with her intoxicating beauty and delicate touch.

He rubbed a weary hand across his face, forcing himself to think about dinner. It was the next item on his list. Eat, then sleep. The only problem was, he could do almost anything and still think about her. It was only by wrestling his thoughts into focus that he could drive her out.

Like a sandwich.

He layered on his favorites—salami and provolone, avocado and tomato, lots of lettuce. And then he thought about his mouth while he ate. About the different textures and tastes. He became a robot, ignoring his heart completely and simply checking off tasks.

His dreams, though, he couldn't control. And they always returned to her. She would be standing in the redwood forest, near the tallest tree, just like every night before. As much as he yelled, she couldn't hear him and only stood searching into the trees like there was something she couldn't quite make out. Then the daylight would flicker, and suddenly, she was standing in front of him, so close they were touching. Her hands grazed his arms and slid around his back, holding him against her tightly. He fought the urge to take her in his arms, but he never knew why. Why couldn't he just let go and hold her the way he wanted to?

But it was a battle with himself, and he would lose,

either way. Because no matter what happened in the dream, he would wake up. And she wouldn't be there.

So, he kept his schedule. His seamless movement from one task to the next, like he was made of pure, relentless dedication instead of the truth... that he hardly felt human anymore.

But ignoring his heart had made things easier, in a muted, lifeless way. It made things easier when Abigail showed up the next week and picked up Champ, taking his crate and food and all his things with her. It made things easier when he finally got that raise; the one that would have paid for their house together. The one he never told her about. It was supposed to be a surprise, but she'd fallen in love with another dream. One that didn't live in a cozy neighborhood with a steady job. A dream that was more than he'd ever imagined, which was likely why they weren't together anymore. Because he couldn't imagine the way she could.

But one week after Champ had gone to live with Abigail, he woke up and something had changed. His dream had been about work. Abigail hadn't appeared once. He sat at the kitchen table, stirring his cereal but never taking a bite. Did it mean he was moving on? Getting over her? Because his heart didn't seem to be getting with the program. It cramped and ached and threatened to make him more emotional than he'd been since he was a child. Like she'd stepped out of the dream and was standing next to him instead.

And he was done aching.

He ignored his breakfast and rushed to the garage where he kept his tools. If there was one thing he knew how to do, it was how to build houses. And since Abigail was torturing his thoughts day and night anyway, he was going to embrace the hurt and make himself useful at the same time. So what if he didn't agree with what she was doing? The huge risk and unknowns she would face wasn't really his problem. But what was his problem was the fact that his life had turned to ashes. Maybe this final act of helping out someone he loved with his whole being would rid him of her ghost. Because anything was better than living with the torture of loving something you didn't have.

In hardly twenty minutes, he was speeding across the Bay Bridge, eyeing the deep green hills of the redwoods and forcing his emotions into check. He was going to work on a house. That was it.

When he finally pulled up to Poppyridge Cove, his mouth dropped open. It looked like a completely different place. Foliage and dead trees had all been cleared away, leaving a smooth, clean worksite with an even more incredible view. Instead of feeling closed in like before, it was sprawling and open, perched atop the world with the ocean at its feet. A few trees had been left to grow, and with the way they'd lived their lives bunched in, it had created artistic winding patterns in the branches and trunks, leaving them posed in graceful arches and bows, somehow perfectly placed.

A work trailer was close by, with a few men standing around it, sipping coffee. They eyed Chase curiously. After another sweep of the site, he spotted a smaller trailer, modern and clean, placed closer to the forest. He recognized Abigail's slippers on the step and a leash hung next to the door. His heart throbbed until he nearly snarled, forcing it to stop. He snatched up his toolbelt from the backseat and stepped out.

The afternoon sun was strong and warm, and a cool breeze blew off the ocean. Mixed in with the heavy pine smell of the redwoods, it was a beautiful harmony. Chase strapped on his tools and walked up to the work trailer. "How're things going?" he asked, ready to jump in and start working. He waited through the awkward pause he'd known was coming. These men had no idea who he was, after all. They no doubt thought he was some greenhorn neighbor who got an early Christmas present from Home Depot. "Has demolition been completed?"

One of the men stepped forward. He had a hardhat on with a symbol on it like he might be someone in charge.

"It has," he said shortly. "Who are you?"

"I'm a friend of the owner. I haven't had time away until now, but I'm ready to get to work." Chase eyed the house again, spotting some siding that was rotted and needed to be stripped away. "I can start on the outside if you want. Looks like there are some rot and damaged areas."

The in-charge man held his hand up. "Hold on now, let's just have you work with a partner for a while here." He clapped Chase on the shoulder. "We're on break, just give us a few minutes."

Chase ground his teeth together, holding back his irritation. "All right," he grumbled, "I'll just take a look around."

He didn't wait for permission and strode up to the house. It had definite potential, with a fountain that was the start of a grand statement. He opened the front door, scanning the doorframe and imagining the resurfacing it would need.

But once inside, Chase stopped analyzing and only stared. It was more elegant than he would have thought from the state of the outside. Something about the layout of the house felt friendly and warm but held on to a firm luxury as well. It was like no house he'd ever seen. Even the sprawling mansions he'd worked on before all boasted their luxury like a treat no one was allowed to taste, but this house... Something about it clutched at his soul, a call from back in time when life was about kindness and experiences.

He walked slowly through, his boots sounding heavy on the solid floors. The ballroom was impressive and elegant, but he continued up the staircase, admiring the railing and feeling a little disappointed in the lack of light and view. He wondered if Abigail had felt the same way or if she liked the more cozy, protected design.

There were more bedrooms than he'd anticipated, but he only glanced in the doorways as he passed until he came to the last one. It was larger and held a sitting area and a wide fireplace along one side. He tried to force the thoughts away, but they persisted. This could have been theirs, together. Him and Abigail.

"Ey, there!" A voice called from downstairs, jerking Chase from his thoughts. He left quickly, ready to get to work.

CHAPTER 15

Abby woke up later than usual, not having been jolted from sleep by the sound of hammers and saws, which meant the workers were either taking too many breaks or they'd finally started on the inside. It took them the entire first week just to clear the area, leaving her feeling frustrated and impatient, although she tried not to show it. Her working relationship with the crew had been great so far, and she wanted to keep it that way.

The first few days Vance had been her shadow, showing up on-site every morning and constantly re-explaining her wishes to the crew to ensure their work was perfection. It got to be a little grating if Abby was being honest. She could explain herself just fine and hated the assumption that she might need him around. She didn't. Secretly she was glad he had so many appointments filling up his days recently.

The morning was nearly slipping into afternoon by the time she left her cozy trailer. Champ bounded down the steps and took off into the forest, where he'd made a habit of exploring each day. But for the most part, he stayed close enough, so Abby didn't mind. She suspected his presence had somehow stopped the appearance of dead animals on the porch.

The first few nights she'd spent in her trailer had been tense. Each morning, a freshly killed animal, head removed, was found on the porch. She made sure to dispose of the creatures and clean up the wood before Vance arrived, so he had no idea. But after Champ had begun exploring the redwoods, it stopped. No animals had been found for the last three days, although today she'd gotten up so late, she wondered if someone might have disposed of an animal without her knowing.

She walked to the house, watching the ground for she didn't know what. Perhaps footprints? A trail of something being dragged? But there was such a large crew on site, it could be anyone or anything. The steps looked clean, as did the deck, and she doubted one of the crew would go so far as to wash off any trace of the animal.

Still, her stomach twisted at the thought. It wouldn't leave her alone until she knew for sure. She pulled the porch screen open with a loud screech, reminding her that it desperately needed to be replaced.

Inside, there was the intermittent communication of construction. Someone called from upstairs and a voice in the kitchen replied just before the crew chief appeared. He gave her an eyebrow-raise of acknowledgment but rushed past. She held a hand up. "Wait—Mark."

"Yes?" He turned but didn't stop, so she rushed out her question loudly.

"Were there any animals on the porch this morning?"

His face contorted in confusion, and there was a pause

before his answer. "Er—no, ma'am." He clomped up the steps, and Abby sighed with relief.

She thought back to the few animals she'd seen recently and wondered just what was going on. After seeing them up close, she knew it wasn't another animal killing them. Their heads had been severed from their bodies with something sharp and smooth. A knife was most likely. But the thought of someone performing such a sickening act over and over... It made the back of her neck tingle.

Through her thoughts, she could hear one of the workers behind her as he walked in the ballroom. His steps were heavy and slow as if he were unsure where he should be. It was an unusual cadence and brought her out of her thoughts enough to have her wondering. She wasn't paying them to waste time. Suddenly, she realized he was coming closer and sounded almost directly behind her. It was such an eerie thought that she spun around.

Chase stopped in his tracks with his eyes locked on hers.

"Chase," she breathed. In the brief silence, she noticed a few things very quickly, like the way he filled out his gray shirt. It was one he used to wear when they went running together, but now it was stretched across his chest in a way it never used to. And he'd obviously been working hard with the way it was clinging to him, nearly transparent; she could make out the ridges of his strong middle quite easily.

Her eyes flickered back to his. "What're you doing here?" She'd wanted to sound stronger, more demanding. But her voice was weak and caught in her throat.

Chase hadn't said a word yet, and he looked perplexed.

Abby suddenly hoped there wasn't a big smudge of dirt on her face. She wished he would turn away for a moment so she could wipe her hand across her skin.

"I…" Chase pulled in an impressive, sweeping breath. "I wanted to come help out. I'm sorry I've been so distant on this project instead of offering my help. I should've done that in the very beginning."

Abby only stared back at him, feeling more confused than before. Hadn't he been completely adamant about *not* helping? Wasn't that part of his ethical stance on the situation? And yet here he was, working with her, and he didn't seem to be holding anything back, judging by his sweaty shirt.

"Thank you," she finally said, realizing it had been quite a long pause. But he had to admit, it was a big change from the adamant way he'd rebelled against her entire decision to fix up the house.

"You're welcome, Abigail."

His voice was soft and sincere, and she looked up into his face, noticing the way his eyes traced over her features. It sent her heart racing, although she tried to hide the flush she knew was overwhelming her cheeks. She smiled quickly. "I have to go find Champ, see you later. Thanks for coming."

"I'll see you later." He turned back to the ballroom, and she meant to turn away too. But instead, she gazed across his back at the strength there, amazed this was the same man she knew a few weeks earlier. He looked incredible. Memories of being held in his arms burst into her mind, and she sand into them easily. The gentle way he moved, how he smelled. Instantly she wholly, desperately, and overwhelmingly wanted it back again.

"Ms. Tanner?"

She jumped, glancing back at Mark. "Yes?"

"You said something about animals?" He shook his head. "Sorry, but I don't know what you're talking about. What kind of animals? And don't you have a trail cam somewhere up there? My roofing guys said they noticed something like that."

The trail-cam!

"Yes, I do. Thank you. I'm sure it won't be a problem anymore."

He nodded and went back to the kitchen. It had been stripped clean, leaving only a few holes in the walls with bunches of wires protruding. He pulled at the nearest bunch and scooped up a set of pliers from the floor.

It was nice to see the work getting done. Abby pulled her phone from her pocket and snapped a quick picture. She wanted the entire project well documented. All except for the grotesque display of animals on the porch—she wished she could rid her memory of every last trace of them.

She marched back to the porch and looked up into the eaves where the camera was still concealed. She'd completely forgotten about it, and for a moment, she wondered if Vance had, too, since he hadn't said a word about it either.

After dragging the tallest ladder she could find back to the deck, she leaned it against the roof, making sure to angle it just right. The feet set into the soft dirt so well, it seemed very stable. She gripped the sides, attempting to shake it. The ladder held firm, so she climbed up quickly and pulled the trail cam from its place. There was a little red light flashing, signifying a low battery.

"Careful, Abby!" Vance shouted from his car, where he'd just pulled up.

In her surprise, she flinched and the ladder lost a bit of its grip. It began to wobble, making her knees shake and her balance waver. She gripped the ladder with one hand, holding the camera in the other. But the ladder slid a bit like it was going to tilt to the side and fall off the roof completely.

"Whoa," she mumbled, trying to hold on with her other hand. Instead, the camera just clunked against the side of the ladder. She could feel it tipping, and she stepped down quickly before she could fall. But the camera slipped from her hand and crashed to the ground.

She reached for it too quickly and lost her balance. The ladder was knocked from her grip and she gasped, sure she was going to land sprawled on the deck like one of those animals.

She tried to get her feet under her and heard some commotion just before landing partially on her feet and partially in Chase's arms. He'd dashed under the ladder just in time and, breathing hard, he stood with his arms around her.

Shocked and gasping, Abby only looked back at him. His eyes were wide with adrenaline, and he glanced across her quickly. "You okay?" he asked, still breathless.

Abby held on to a strong arm and shoulder as she got herself onto her feet. But she wasn't ready to leave his arms just yet. She could tell he was about to let her go, seeing that she was standing on her own. But she made sure to keep her hands tightly holding on to him, not stepping away from their closeness.

He seemed to notice, and his head turned back slowly.

"Thank you," she whispered. Even when her heart was pounding so loudly she was sure the whole house could hear it, her voice managed to be buttery-soft.

His face calmed, and he moved one hand gently to her back, leaning closer, ever so slowly.

"That was close, Abby! Are you okay?" Vance came barging in with his loud words, making them both jump.

Chase glanced longingly across her face once more before stepping back and releasing her.

Abby felt plunged in ice water. After finally being so close to him again only to be ripped apart, her head was swimming.

Vance squeezed her in a tight hug so quickly she hardly had time to react. He stepped back and smacked Chase on the shoulder. "You were in the right place, that's for sure. Great job, man."

Chase stiffened a bit, his eyes glancing at Vance's hand still on her shoulder. "Yeah," he answered, "glad I got here in time."

"Do you think the trail cam is broken, Abbs?" Vance asked, using the nickname he'd made up that she completely hated. She wished she'd told him that the very first time he'd used it. Now that it had been a few days, it was going to be more awkward to tell him the truth. He bent down to investigate, and Abby looked back at Chase.

He was staring at her almost coldly, and she nearly flinched. What was going on with him? She was sure he'd been about to kiss her, and now? Now he looked angry.

"You don't need to feel obligated to help here, Chase," she said quietly, although it still sounded rude even in her own ears.

Vance even glanced between them for a moment before returning to his study of the trail cam.

"I assure you, I don't feel obligated," Chase replied. "I just know how much work this will take."

Abby tried not to let his words set her off. She tried to hide the angry warmth that was spreading into her face. But she was sure Chase could tell. He knew her well enough to realize what he was saying—that she wasn't capable of doing this without him. And she resented him for that. It was a devastating twist in her emotions to want him so badly one moment, and the next, she was trying not to ball her hand into a fist.

"I'd better get back." Chase turned and pulled open the screen with a screech, disappearing into the ballroom again.

Abby hadn't even had time to reply. She wanted to tell him she was fine on her own—happy even. She didn't need anyone else. But she'd be lying even to herself. The truth was, she missed him every day. The pain that was spreading through her chest was excruciating, and she worked to fight it off… just in time for Vance to stand up with the camera in one hand.

"Where'd you put the charger?" he asked. "I think it'll still work if we just get it charged."

Abby snatched it from his hand. "I'll do it," she answered, heading back to her trailer quickly enough to relay the message that she didn't want company.

She hurled herself up the tiny steps and inside her trailer and let the door slam behind her. Breathing hard, her hands were trembling. Whatever was going on inside her, it felt close to destruction. She was still dizzy from being in his arms, but anger had somehow pushed away whatever affection she'd felt only minutes before.

Their relationship had never been like this. Not once in their two years together had she been anything more than perhaps a little irritated, and that was usually on a bad day, anyway. And when they'd kissed before, it had been enjoyable, but never had she felt nearly faint in his arms. Never had she been so desperate for him to be close to her. Her heart was still pounding, and her anger was bordering on tears.

It was all so confusing. This was Chase! The dependable, rational guy who was always well prepared. Was it just his new physique that was setting her off so much? Was she that shallow? Still, it was the only thing she could think of that had changed.

Abby walked to the counter and plugged in the trail cam. If his newly built self was causing so much trouble inside her, at least she realized now what the problem was. She just needed to concentrate on something else and not let herself admire him quite so much.

There.

Problem solved.

The small camera beeped, and the screen flickered to life. It had been activated a few times, and she rewound the footage quickly, anxious to finally discover the mystery of her porch. She pushed play and felt immediately disappointed. The screen was streaked with disruption, likely from when she'd dropped it to the deck. Static flickered across it constantly, but she squinted her eyes and peered through it.

At first, it was just a bird landing on the deck and pecking at it for a few minutes. It seemed the angle was off, providing a view of the door and deck more than the surrounding property in front of it like she'd wanted. Someone could sneak right up to the stairs without triggering the camera. She grumbled to herself about letting Vance install it. But he'd seemed so confident, like he'd done it a hundred times before.

Then the last video flickered on, and a few leaves brushed their way across the wood planks. Abby exhaled in a gust of disappointment until something big and furry flopped into view. An arm was outstretched, visible to about the elbow before it retreated. She gasped, erupting into chills across her legs, arms, and neck.

It had been a man's arm, although lean. The picture was so fuzzy not much else was visible. But there was a man on her property, feet from where she'd been sleeping in her trailer. He'd killed an animal and left it on her porch.

She glanced at the time on the screen. 4 a.m. It sunk in slowly that this was real, and her throat began to feel strangled. She'd been foolishly sleeping out in the forest alone while some creeper was sneaking around—it was terrifying.

A knock on her door had her jumping back from the camera in shock. It hung from the cord, dangling off the counter.

"Abigail?" Chase's voice was soft, like he wasn't sure he wanted an answer. Maybe he was just feeling guilty and needed to clear his conscience.

She tried to calm down but was still breathing hard when the door inched open.

"What's going on?" Chase asked, entering cautiously.

He stopped when he looked at her face, appearing unsure of how to continue. "Is Vance here?"

Abby shook her head in confusion. Why would Vance be in her trailer?

Chase glanced at the camera and back at Abby before lifting it to the countertop. All Abby could think of was his arms around her. She closed her eyes, willing herself to stop thinking.

"May I?"

Her eyes flickered open and she nodded, watching with him as the same footage repeated. Only this time, when the arm appeared, she nearly jumped to the ceiling.

Chase glanced back at her with concern lining his face. It made her eyes water and threatened to have her stepping into his safe embrace again.

"Abby, you can't stay here," he said seriously.

"I don't—" Her voice caught, and she shrugged, not wanting to finish that sentence. She didn't have anywhere else to go. This was now her home.

Chase turned back to the camera and rewound it. After only a few seconds, he paused the screen, studying the blurry arm more closely. He tapped at the image. "This is a tattoo," he said quietly. Abby inched closer and leaned in next to him, recognizing the dark design just above the wrist on the inside of the arm.

"Can you tell what it is?" She squinted, trying to make it out.

"I don't know… looks like stars, maybe?" Chase's voice was deep and close and sounded like pure comfort. Abby wanted to wrap herself in all its smooth, creamy tones.

She quickly reminded herself that she was only being

shallow and took a few steps back, making sure to keep her eyes on the trail cam. Nothing else.

"I'd better get back to work," Chase said. "I just wanted to apologize for earlier. That was rude of me."

Abby glanced up. Before she'd seen the video, she would have wanted to dig into this conversation and let him know she was completely capable on her own. But all her confidence felt shattered, and she just wanted him to stay. "No, it's okay, Chase." She hadn't meant to say his name so sincerely, and his eyes lifted to meet hers as if it had surprised him as well. The seconds that passed felt genuine and personal.

"Let me know if you need anything," Chase finally said, breaking the silence as he scooted out the small door.

Abby felt completely out of touch with her own emotions as well as his. It was strange to have no idea what his expressions meant and to hold back when she had something to say. It was like their relationship remained strung together by a single thread. Too weak to last through anything major, and yet neither of them wanted to break it.

CHAPTER 16

The night had been more sleepless than any Abby could recall. She'd even let Champ snuggle up at the bottom of her bed, a habit she'd spent weeks training him out of. But there seemed to be more crackling branches and whistling wind than any night before. Even the sound of the ocean was suddenly hostile and intimidating. It was a relief when the curtains were illuminated with the first of the morning light.

"C'mon Champ," Abby said, rubbing the groggy puppy's head. He seemed confused to be up so early, but it only lasted half a second. The next moment he was on the floor, padding around excitedly with his tail whipping everything around him with a strong *thwap, thwap*.

She loved their usual morning walk, although it had never been quite this early. The forest still looked dark and mysterious. Champ bounded out the door, and Abby reached for his leash but stopped when she saw Champ had frozen with his legs stiff, and the hair on his back bristling. With her heart racing, she spun around and scanned the area. Along the porch, she could just make out a lump of fur.

Suddenly, twigs snapped behind the trees, and bushes rustled as if something were forcing its way through. Abby gasped and called for Champ as she dashed back up the steps. The puppy raced inside and she closed the door, twisting the feeble lock and staring with wide eyes at the door. The bushes were still rustling, and Abby fumbled with her phone, breathing hard. She hoped the construction crew would pull up soon, but until then, there was only one phone number she could think of.

"Bee?" His voice was groggy and filled with sleep. She hadn't heard him call her Bee in a long time. All her fear came out in a rush.

"There's another animal on the porch!" she paused and gasped in a few breaths.

"What?"

"I saw it, and I can hear something in the forest. I thought Champ had scared away whatever was bringing the animals, but then we saw that video, and it's not an animal—" Her words cut off when something bumped the trailer. Her fear lodged in her throat. "Chase, there's someone here," she squeaked, forcing the words out.

"Hang up and call the police," he urged, "I'm on my way."

Champ, who'd been curled up at her feet, suddenly stood and faced the door. A low growl rumbled in his throat. She pushed the emergency button on her phone with shaking hands and clung to the device while it rang.

"Hello, rescue 911, what's your emergency?"

The door to the trailer rattled like someone was trying to open it, and Abby's voice lodged in her throat.

"Can you state your emergency, please?"

Champ growled and barked, still frozen in place. The rattling stopped. "Abbs?" The sound of Vance's voice had her releasing all her breath at once.

"I'm sorry—everything's okay," she stuttered, "thank you."

She set her hand on Champ's back and he jerked, swinging his head around. "It's okay, boy."

"Vance?" she called, with fear still pulsing through her veins.

"Yeah—everything all right in there?"

Abby twisted the lock and pulled the door open, letting Vance step through.

His eyes surveyed the place as if it might be on fire. With one look at her face, he pulled her into a hug. "What's going on?" he asked.

She was sure he could feel her whole body trembling. It nearly knocked her off her feet, and she clung to him, struggling to catch her breath. Relief covered her like a blanket, but it also made her so weak she could hardly answer.

"Someone—was here," she breathed, resting her head on his chest and trying to shake the nerves.

"I came out early," he answered, with his hand resting on her head. "And I'm glad I did. There wasn't anyone else out there, but some kind of animal was scratching around your trailer. It was big, looked like a dang wolverine! Do you have wolverines out here?" He leaned away from her, and she let her arms drop, finally putting her fears into perspective.

It was just an animal?

"No, we don't have wolverines," she answered, beginning to feel foolish. "Did you see what was on the porch?"

Vance turned and glanced behind them, "Ah, so it happened again." He turned back to her and lifted his hand to her face, brushing her hair aside. But his hand lingered there, tracing her jaw slowly. "I'll get rid of it for you, don't worry."

His hand steadily moved to her neck, and she stepped away. But he moved in closer and slid his hand to her back, bringing them together. "Wait," he whispered, lowering his head until his lips brushed hers.

She turned her head, still reeling with the aftertaste of so much adrenaline. "Don't, Vance." She breathed, bringing her hands to his chest. She pushed against him gently, waiting for him to step away. But he didn't.

"Give me a chance, Abby," he pleaded, bringing both his hands to her face and leaning over her again.

Strength burst open inside of her, and she shoved him away. "Stop!" she demanded, just as a car pulled up to the house with its tires skidding in the gravel.

Vance glanced behind them and turned back to her with anger on his face. "Fine, after everything I've done for you, just go ahead and brush me off." He left the trailer, stomping down the steps.

Abby followed quickly with her cheeks burning, but she refused to let him accuse her. "What does that mean?" she asked, grabbing his arm.

He stopped and spun around. All the kindness had disappeared from his manners, turning his usually approachable features into something almost frightening. He jerked her hand away.

"I hired you to help me purchase this house," she continued, "which I've done. I don't owe you anything."

He didn't look like he was going to answer, but after a long moment of glaring back at her, he finally did. "So, all that time you spent flirting with me was just for this house? I get it now."

Abby's mouth dropped open. She snapped it shut and ground her teeth together. "I don't want you coming back here, not even to help," she warned, keeping her eyes steady as he glared at her.

A car door closed and footsteps pressed through the dirt.

"I won't," Vance snapped, swishing a hand up as if he were waving away an unpleasant smell. "Good luck with this dump." He turned and strode past Chase, who eyed him suspiciously and twisted around to watch him start up his car and spin the tires in his haste to back out.

When his car shot down the road and turned out of sight, Chase finally turned back to Abby. His shirt was hanging at an awkward angle, and his hair was still ruffled on one side from sleep. "What happened?" he asked. His voice was groggy. He hesitated and shifted his weight from foot to foot. "Was he the one sneaking around your trailer?"

"I—no, it was an animal, I guess." Abby turned and looked back at her trailer. Champ was sniffing the ground close by, looking very captivated by something. "I didn't see it, but I heard it."

"And there's another animal on your porch," Chase said. He walked back to peer at the decapitated critter.

When Abby came closer, she could see it was a raccoon. A young one.

"Maybe the mother wasn't happy about her baby being taken," Chase suggested. "Racoons can be pretty vicious. They've even been known to attack humans when threatened."

Abby shrugged, still reeling from the shock of earlier and the confusion of Vance. "I suppose," she answered, feeling completely uninterested in the habits of raccoons.

If only Vance had never shown up that day, and Chase was the one to come to her trailer. She eyed him as he looked down at the porch. He must have rushed out in a hurry, judging by the sleep on his face. But the way he was acting now, it hardly seemed like he'd been worried. He kept glancing back at the road like he was expecting Vance to return.

Champ circled them and trotted off to the trees, where he liked to explore most of the day. Chase watched him silently until he was out of sight. "Do you worry about Champ?" he asked.

Abby shook her head. "Oh no, he's okay. He likes to explore the forest. It's fine, he knows the way."

"I'm sure he does," Chase answered, "but do you think it's safe? I mean, he's not much bigger than a lot of these animals you've found on your porch."

Abby's eyes widened, and she searched the trees until she saw his tail whipping back and forth behind a bush. "I hadn't even thought of that," she admitted, with chills covering her arms. Who would ever want to hurt a puppy?

"Champ!" she called.

His head lifted from the foliage and he charged back, racing the entire way until he was at their feet.

"I've got a fairly long rope. I guess I could tie him up." Abby felt guilty already. "I know he won't like it."

Chase rubbed the puppy's head and sighed. "Yeah, he probably won't. But it's not forever. Just until you get this figured out, right?" He smiled back at her, lifting his eyebrows and looking as optimistic as she'd ever seen.

"Right," she answered, trying to give him a confident smile as well. But in the back of her mind, she was wondering what it would take to stop someone from delivering these animal carcasses to her door. Just what did they expect her to do about it?

* * *

IT WAS HALFWAY through the afternoon, and Abby had skipped lunch. She sipped on some cocoa the workers had brought in a plastic drum, just hot enough for the chilly, overcast day. She tipped the cup back and finished the last drop just as Mark, the project manager, joined her.

"I got some news for you, Ms. Tanner," he began, lifting a hand up. "Now, it's not bad, but it's not great either."

Abby nodded, ready for the worst.

"The plumbing needs to go. We can keep the older fixtures if you'd like, but we've gotta dig pretty deep to pull up some of the pipe. It's rotting clean away."

"Oh." Abby sighed, glad it wasn't something worse. They'd already spoken about the possible need for new plumbing, and it didn't seem like a very big surprise.

"What I need you to do," he continued, "Is to let the neighbors know. There's gonna be some long, loud days ahead, and it's best to try to smooth things over ahead of time. I've got a job description and some contact information printed up that you can give them, but usually just a considerate conversation is all it takes."

"I'd be happy to." Abby smiled, grateful for the task.

"Great." Mark glanced at the house like he was itching to get back to work. "I left the papers in the cab of the truck." He tapped the tailgate. "I thought you'd find them here fairly easily since you seem to enjoy a cup of cocoa." He winked and reached for a tool from his belt as he walked away.

"Thanks, Mark," Abby called, laughing at his observations. He was spot on. She refilled her cup and went to retrieve the papers.

Walking down the street was rejuvenating with the tall pine trees and their deep, beautiful colors. It made everything around them look alive with adventure.

The first house was the Allens, where she'd had lunch before. She knocked quietly and waited. They were retired, but she guessed they traveled a lot, so maybe they weren't even going to be around for the "loud days" as Mark had called them.

After a couple of minutes, she rang the doorbell and leaned over to peer in through a long side window. It was immaculate, just like she'd remembered. But no one came to the door. She rolled the paper up and slid it through the handle.

The next house was empty as well, and after it was the one Abby had been wanting to visit, especially after hearing the Allens teasingly call them *ramboisterous*. She knocked. There was only silence inside, and no window to look through, but she waited while she imagined a person on crutches, slowly making their way to the door.

But after even an invalid length of time, there was still nothing.

"Okay," she mumbled, leaving the note rolled into their handle yet again. The next house, she already knew, was usually vacant. Apparently, the owners were only around occasionally. She rang the doorbell anyway and left the note rolled up.

When she reached the last house with the friendly old man she'd seen before, she could make out someone at the kitchen table. There was a scramble of noise on the sidewalk behind her, and she spun around to see Champ racing to meet her with his tongue lolling out.

She snatched at his collar just as the door opened. The puppy whined and squirmed, wanting to say hello to the woman who had just opened the door. She didn't look much older than Abby.

"Hello." Abby tried to control Champ for a moment. "I'm sorry, my dog got loose," she explained, just as Chase ran up to join her, breathing harder than Champ had been.

"Sorry about that," he huffed. "I let him off for a bit to run, and he ran." He chuckled, and the woman at the door laughed with him.

"It's no problem," she said. "Was there something you needed?"

"Yes." Abby waited for Chase to clip on the leash and finally let go of the excited puppy. "I'm your new neighbor down the street, at the Poppyridge house. We're going to be pulling out some old plumbing, and I wanted to let you know ahead of time."

The woman took the paper Abby held out and glanced down at it as she spoke. "Oh, thank you. But I don't live here, my dad does. I came down to help because he was sick for a few days," She glanced up and saw Abby's concerned face. "But he's doing much better now," she assured.

"Someone at the door, hun?" A voice called from inside the house.

"Yeah, Dad, it's your neighbor," the woman answered.

"Oh!" The older man appeared, smiling back at them. "How nice to see you again." He shook both their hands. "Don't know if I introduced myself before. I'm Harold, hello."

"Hi," Abby said, "we've been working on repairs, and I wanted to give you guys a little warning."

"Oh, nothing wrong I hope?" Harold asked. "We've been anxious to see the place finished. It's about time someone took it on." He paused with his eyes twinkling, "It's a good thing you're young—that project isn't for the faint of heart." He chuckled at his joke, just like he had the first time they'd met.

"You're right about that." Chase laughed. Abby smiled along with them, quickly distracted by Chase's pleasant face and the way he genuinely enjoyed other people. He was a lot like Champ. The comparison made her grin… until she noticed no one was laughing anymore.

"Well," she continued, handing out the paper. The young woman stepped aside so her father could take it. "It will be a bit noisy for the next few days, so we wanted to give you a little notice and let you know who to contact if you need anything."

"Thank you, but I'm sure it'll be fine," Harold said, glancing down at the paper. "I appreciate the concern though. You'll make very nice neighbors."

He glanced between Abby and Chase, and for an awkward second, Abby wondered if she should correct him. But the moment passed, and Chase didn't jump in either, so she let it go.

"Feel free to stop by anytime," Harold added, with his eyes pulling down a bit, leaving him looking like a sad puppy—like Champ when he was tied up.

Abby assured him they would, and they shook his hand again in parting, but as they turned to leave, the young woman scooted out the door with them. "I'm just heading to the market," she explained. "I'll walk with you—bye, Pop!"

She walked alongside Abby until the door had closed. "I just needed to tell you something before you go." She glanced back at the house and lowered her voice. "I appreciate you guys coming out and taking the time to say hello to my dad. He's had a really hard time since my mom passed away a couple of years ago, and it's a two-hour drive for me to be here. I've been trying to get him to move in with me, but he loves it here. So, I just wanted to tell you thanks. He really could use a little attention from a neighbor." Her eyes became misty. "You two are so sweet. I can just feel your goodness, and I wanted to share that with you. Please keep an eye on him for me. I have to be heading home tomorrow."

Her comments made Abby's eyes cloudy too, and she hugged her quickly. "We'll be sure to check in on him often," she promised. "But we never got your name."

"Oh, I'm sorry." The girl laughed. "I'm so forgetful—runs in the family. I'm Jess." She smiled at them and turned to her car. "Thanks again!" she called.

Chase lifted a hand and waved goodbye before his eyes

dropped to Abby. She was sure he could see the emotion there, the way it was clouding her vision. And it wasn't just because Jess had confided in them, it was more than that. The way both she and Harold had assumed they were building the house together, as a couple. It left her feeling devastated that they weren't.

Chase kept glancing back at her face as they walked, but she didn't feel in the mood to explain. "This is a beautiful place." He was looking up the hill, where the house had just come into view, and the sun had chased away the cloud cover. It streamed down on the wet landscape with the ocean just peeking out on one side.

It was beautiful. Abby smiled and blinked away any additional moisture in her eyes. "It's incredible," she agreed. It was nice to hear him say something good about the place. She was pretty sure he still thought she was crazy for buying it. "I can't explain it, but there's something here that speaks to me, like it was always waiting here… just for me."

She would have said more, like how her heart burned in her chest every time she'd visited as if she'd burst with happiness. Or how she saw visions of a future she never dreamed was possible for her, but only when she was here. It was a type of magic she wanted more of. But she couldn't risk him chasing those visions away. She glanced up to see him watching her.

"Well, you seem happy here, I can't deny that." He smiled softly, but it was brief. "Have you called the police about this morning? I mean, it could have been a raccoon, but who knows for sure?"

She hesitated, not wanting to talk about it.

"If you want to feel completely comfortable here Abby,

you need to get this figured out." He stopped and rested a hand on her shoulder. She tried not to let him see how much it affected her, leaving her skin tingling at the weight of his hand. "Someone is sneaking onto your property and leaving dead animals behind. It's morbid. And whoever is doing it, they need to be arrested."

He dropped his hand and she sighed. He was right. "I'll call them right now," she promised.

Chase looked like he was going to get back to work from the way he studied the house and tightened the toolbelt hanging around his jeans.

Abby wondered if the other men noticed the difference in appearances and the way Chase was more like an advertisement for tools, or jeans, or aftershave. He looked back at her, and she flinched.

"Here," she said, reaching for the leash, "I'll take Champ back." There was a lot more she needed to say, especially with the way her heart was pounding. But Chase looked preoccupied and was no doubt making a list of things he wanted to get finished for the day.

"Okay," he said, still distracted by his study of the house, "I'll see you later."

"Bye." Abby made sure to turn and walk away decidedly—swiftly—nearly running. It was the only way she could stop herself from confessing her feelings for him in a big, mushy display. He was sure to disappear forever if she did that.

CHAPTER 17

The police reacted just as Abby thought they would. No doubt they were pushing the mute button to keep from laughing in her face. But eventually, they did agree to send someone out. The animal had been cleaned up, but after seeing footage from the trail-cam, the officer was advised to watch the property overnight. He didn't look happy about it, either.

Abby knocked on his window with a cup of cocoa in one hand. "Thought you might like some hot chocolate," she offered, handing him the cup.

He smiled but didn't seem in the mood for conversation.

"I can't thank you enough for keeping me safe tonight," she added, feeling a little dramatic but completely real at the same time.

The officer's eyes lifted to hers, and he seemed to see her differently. He nodded. "Whatever I can do, miss. It's my job."

She left it at that, not wanting to push their newly cordial relationship.

It had been weeks since she'd changed her mailing address, but she hadn't received a single letter yet. When she caught sight of the mailbox, she knew she'd finally been located. It was on a beautiful sturdy post stained to match the stone and wood pillars she was having built at the front and back of the house. And a miniature beach house had been specially ordered as her mailbox. It was a little whimsical, but it fit her dreams nicely.

The front of the box had popped open a little, showing at least a dozen letters and magazines tucked inside. She pulled them out in a heap and spotted five gold envelopes. It set her heart racing, and she hurried back to her trailer, wanting to open them as quickly as possible.

Settling down at the small table, she set everything else aside. The envelopes were first. After opening each one, she organized them chronologically and started with #3. It was a beautiful little request to write her future self a letter as if the next ten years had already happened. Easy enough. She moved on.

#4. Open an investment account.

This one had her pausing, as it was completely different from the previous three. Instead of allowing any creative license, it was a solid definition of what needed to be done. Fine.

#5. Another poetic paragraph made up of only a few lines, but Abby couldn't stop reading it over and over, until her head could process what needed to be done. To visit her mother's grave and leave flowers.

It felt like a rock had replaced her stomach, or all her insides completely. She hadn't been to the cemetery since her funeral, and even that had been a strange kind of torture. To honor someone who had nearly killed her with neglect. She wiped at the perspiration on her forehead and flipped to the next letter.

#6. Which seemed like part two of #5 and just as crushing. To forgive the one you blame the most.

It was obvious to Abby who that was, but the request seemed mocking in its simplicity. Forgive her? Just like that? She pushed the letter aside and reached for the next.

#7. To love the one you're afraid to love.

Abby's heart felt too overwhelmed to continue. She could hardly breathe through the emotions battling for attention. Why couldn't the mailman have found her earlier, so she didn't have to read all of these at once? Just one drop of poison at a time, please.

There was a light knock on her door, and she lifted her head from the scatter of envelopes. Like little pieces of her heart, ripped off and flung about the table.

"Bee?" Chase's voice was quiet and sincere, a kindness she knew so well it hurt.

She brought one hand to her chest, trying to calm the pain throbbing inside so she could answer. But her eyes had filled with tears, so quickly she knew she was losing the battle.

"You there?" he asked again, more quietly this time.

Abby walked to the door, already knowing she couldn't open it. Not when she had lost all control. Her tears bubbled over and streamed down her cheeks as she rested a hand against the door, taking a quiet breath. If only she hadn't opened those horrible letters.

The steps squeaked as he walked away, leaving her

feeling cold and alone. Champ's collar jingled and she could hear Chase laugh. "Hey, hey—"

She moved carefully to the small window in the kitchen and watched Chase sidestep around Champ, pushing his shoulder playfully and dashing away again. The puppy bounced and twisted, whining and panting in an excited flurry. It made her heart ache even more.

She stepped closer to watch, and Chase's head lifted, staring right at her. He looked suddenly pained, and she realized she was a mess of tears and sorrow. And now he knew she'd ignored him.

She backed away quickly, wiped at her wet cheeks and stacked the wretched gold envelopes together quickly, doing her best to shake off the shock.

Number three. She'd start there and think of nothing else. It was easy enough, after all. Her mind was eager to imagine all her dreams coming true in the next ten years. What she wanted most, at the moment, seemed impossibly out of reach, but the challenge didn't say it had to be rational.

She started with Chase, describing in detail their perfect, affectionate relationship. She poured her heart into the words, confessing her complete adoration of him, and his kindness and attention, and how much she loved him. They had a little boy, and of course, he was a mini-Chase. Blonde, shaggy hair and a big smile that got him out of trouble every day.

Their inn was completed, filled with guests and decorations and holiday cheer. People would come once and return year after year, making it an instant tradition. No sorrow lingered. Fear was only a memory. And regret never made it past the front gate. It was perfect.

She paused and bit her lip before quickly scribbling out the rest. The part where she forgave her mother and was grateful for the life she grew up with, which felt like the most made-up part of the whole thing.

Sealed in a plain white envelope, she tucked it behind the stack of gold envelopes, wondering if she'd have to send a copy to Mr. Blakney or if he would just accept her word that it was written.

If only Vance hadn't hit on her, she could request that he find a sensible investment account and set it up. Instead, she pulled out her phone and called her bank, intending to go with whatever they suggested. She wasn't expecting to be transferred from department to department, only to be left on hold.

Quickly rambled out, in known and foreign words alike, he told her she needed to make the first payment to her mortgage within a month, and it was a substantial amount. The only way she'd be able to pay it would be to obtain the rest of her inheritance. Then, when the money from renters started coming it, the inn would be able to pay for itself. But she hadn't expected the payment to be due so soon.

"I thought the terms of our contract were—"

"Ma'am, I've already listed the terms to you quite clearly. I'm sorry if you misunderstood before. We are going to need the first payment, or we will be take steps to cancel your contract."

Abby felt suddenly dizzy. "I'll have an additional inheritance soon. Is there any way to push the date back?"

He grunted into the phone indignantly. "I'm sorry, but in our line of business, money you don't have is nothing more than money you don't have. We will need the payment in our account or our hands by the end of the month."

She sighed, although her heart was beginning to beat faster. "Okay, I understand. I'll get it to you."

"Thank you, ma'am." He sounded like he was going to hang up, so she asked quickly.

"Also, I wanted a recommendation on an investment account... please."

"For what?" he asked, sounding nearly mocking.

"Investing," she grumbled.

"Let me transfer you."

"No, don't—"

The line disconnected and polite music played quietly. She was on hold. Although she groaned, a dull panic was beginning to tighten in her chest. The possibility that she could lose the house was terrifying. She shook her head, clearing away the fear.

There were only a few more challenges left to receive, even if the ones she'd been given were huge. But how could she just rush through them? She squeezed her eyes shut and let resolve build up inside her, knowing she was going to have to try. Losing the house wasn't an option.

A dull voice answered the phone, and she took their first recommendation, quickly transferring $1,000 into her new account and hanging up as quickly as she could. She was going to race through the challenges and procure the inheritance money; that was all there was to it.

Her hands shook as she thought of number five, but she pulled on her tennis shoes and hurried out the door. The cemetery was over an hour away, so she wanted to get going. Champ jumped up when he saw her, but he sobered quickly, seeming to decipher her nerves.

"Sorry, boy." She rubbed his head. "I'll let you off when I get back."

She rushed past the house, trying to catch her breath while her hands wouldn't stop shaking. Somehow, she had to find the strength—she had to do it. From the corner of her eye, she saw the patio door open as she passed, but she didn't slow down. She wanted to get this over with while she had the courage.

"Abby!" Chase shouted just as she'd opened her car door.

She turned reluctantly, feeling everything inside of her soften at the sight of him. He walked forward slowly, although his eyes were a blaze of energy, holding her gaze captive. His mouth opened but no words came out, and he closed it again, shifting his weight as if he didn't know what to say.

"Uh, the inside's looking great." He fidgeted some more. "They're going to start cutting for those new windows tomorrow. I think that's a great addition. An inspired idea."

He smiled back at her, and she took a deep breath, trying to stop the shaking in her hands. But they still trembled.

"That's great to hear," she said, suddenly wishing he could go with her. If Chase were there, standing beside her at her mother's grave, things would be okay. "I just need to run…" She gestured to her car but couldn't finish her thought out loud. Instead, her eyes slowly wandered back to his. *I have to visit my mother's grave, and I need you there with me.*

Even in her thoughts, it was difficult. How could she ask him?

"Ey, new guy!" A rough voice yelled from inside the house.

Chase turned and held a hand up briefly. When he looked back at Abby, his lips lifted into a crooked apology. "I'd better go finish with the kitchen fixtures." He took a small step and paused, watching her face.

"Oh, yeah," She nodded decidedly. "Go ahead. I've gotta run too, I'll be back later tonight." Her next breath wheezed through her lungs as she watched him walk back to the house.

She was on her own.

* * *

THE DRIVE WENT QUICKLY, although she still felt like she was in some kind of mystical haze. A dream she hadn't entirely woken from, one where anything could happen. Like pulling off the road onto a shadowy lane, where willow trees hung in great weeping displays and tombstones littered the ground.

She stepped from her car and listened to the silence, remembering. The path to her mother's tombstone was easy to trace with her eyes. An invisible trail that had been seared into her memories. She walked it slowly, paying attention to the names she passed to keep one name from her mind.

But when she reached the small gravesite at the edge of the property, she allowed her eyes to settle on its mark. Etched into the gray stone, Loretta Mackay Tanner.

"Hello, Mother," she whispered. It was a beautiful name, she'd always thought. But now all it brought her was pain. Memories of being a child full of hurt and aching, longing for love when all she received was bitterness and cruelty.

She ground her teeth together, fighting the ghosts of the past until it was too much. With a sob, she sunk to her knees, wishing things had somehow been different, and she could say she was sobbing from a heart broken with love lost, or a sweet and tender bond now obsolete.

But it was only the desperate plea of *why*. It crushed her lungs and clenched at her heart with a grip cold and painful. *Why didn't you love me? Why wasn't I enough?* A child again, with no understanding and only tears.

It felt like years that she knelt hunched over in pain, reliving the worst of her life. But after the wave of sorrow passed, the pain eased. For the first time in her life, she felt a cool, soothing spring bubble up from somewhere inside. Like it had opened up in the center of her soul and washed clean the memories of the past. With a deep, cleansing breath, she sat back on her heels. Her heart swelled, a strength and happiness like she'd never known slowly engulfed her. The pain still tinted the edges of her mind, but it no longer hurt.

She thought of Chase, of the forest, the Poppyridge house, her puppy, and everything together. Gently, she settled three white roses atop her mother's grave. A symbol of purity and cleanliness, a fresh start.

She set one hand along the gravestone and was about to stand when her fingers caught on an edge of paper. Fumbling with it, she pinched the object and pulled it from a tangle of bushes that hugged the tombstone.

She stared in shock. It was an envelope with her name, Abigail Tanner, artfully scrawled on the front. Written in pen, the letters had nearly faded away as if it had been waiting years for her to find it.

The glue separated easily as she slid one finger underneath and peered inside. One simple lined paper, yellowed with age, and a small white note were folded together. She lifted them out and opened the note first, recognizing the writing immediately.

— I found this among the small box of possessions that was mailed to me after her death. It's something you need to see with your own eyes. While there was no excuse for her addictions, there was also no doubt of her love for you, my dear niece.

— With love,

Aunt Sharalyn

With hands again shaking, she unfolded the larger note. A full-page, written in pencil and with an unsteady hand. A hand that was likely tremoring with craving.

— My dearest daughter,

You are, to me, something so pure and clean. I recognize it, but I can't be near it. I'm no longer your mother but a demon. The woman who bore you, devoured by a beast that rules the full vessel of what was once a caring human. Now I am neither. It's only at the mercy of this evil being that I watch you suffer, under what looks like my own hand. I cannot be satisfied by anything other than what the demon craves, and its meals lurk in dark corners.

No tender feeling can penetrate its desire, no love can reason with it. I hardly know what love means anymore. I wish to die, so that you may be rid of me, my sweet girl. I loathe the voice that demeans you, the hand that cheats you, the life you must struggle through. But if one day you find it in your heart to no longer hate me, I will be satisfied. It's more than I should ever ask, but in this small moment of clarity, I grasp at this hope like a last gasp for air.

And if you should ever forgive me, you would be truly angelic, my little one.

— With stained hands,
Your mother

It felt like her heart would break in two with her memories now intertwined in her mother's words. But while her vision blurred, her mind was achingly clear with thoughts of a woman overcome with addiction, giving up on life and everything—*everyone* around her. It was shameful and horrid, but also tragic.

For a fleeting moment, Abby could see a tiny glimpse of a world where her mother was healthy, smiling, and kind. Like a glimpse into heaven. And then it was gone.

She folded the papers carefully, stuffing them back in the envelope. When she stood, it was as if all her pain had simply shrugged off and fallen to the ground at her feet. Suddenly she was free, facing the future with no injuries from her past. She could hear the birds in the trees and chipmunks chittering away. Even the damp fall leaves, as they left their high perch and floated a lazy circle until touching the ground. It all seemed connected, harmonious, and something had changed inside.

"I forgive you, Mother," she whispered. A cool breeze rushed past, clearing away the rotting leaves and bringing with it a sweet, clean scent of winter.

CHAPTER 18

When Abby returned to the property, Chase could see something about her had changed. She'd been strangely nervous and upset before, but now... now she looked serene.

He was glad because quite a few things had happened since she left.

He met her at her car and hardly gave her time to say hello before he started explaining. But he was taking his cues from her, and she looked like she was in a great mood.

"So, I just wanted to let you know they only needed to replace one pipe. The others are in great condition, which is amazing. They might even finish up with most of the work today."

Her expression lifted, and a smile spread across her face. It was the content sort of smile he hadn't seen from her in a while.

"I let the neighbors know," he continued, "the Allens and Mr. Fillmore. They both seemed very happy about it."

"That's great!" Abby said, flashing her smile again.

Chase tried to keep his heart in check, but if she kept smiling like that, he was going to throw all caution to the wind and just kiss her. But the way she stepped out and then leaned against her car, she looked exhausted.

"I'm glad to hear it." She sighed. She held an envelope in her hand, opened, with a couple of papers visible inside.

"Where were you?" he asked, feeling curious enough that he didn't mind prying. He'd never seen her quite like she was now. She looked so much stronger but drained at the same time.

Her eyes roamed over him for a moment, and eventually, she pushed off the hood of her car, standing a little closer to him… which he noticed intensely.

"I went to visit my mother's grave," she said quietly.

He knew what this meant. The few moments of her childhood she'd risked sharing with him were utterly dark and shocking. He'd always wished he knew her back then so he could've helped her, and now he understood her smile. It must have taken so much from her, judging by her exhaustion.

He couldn't stop himself from reaching for her, and when he did, she stepped into his arms easily, like she'd been waiting for it. Her arms around him were something he'd dreamed countless times since they'd split up, and he counted the seconds, knowing it wouldn't last long and wishing she would stay there forever.

But instead of letting go, she turned her head, leaning it against his chest as she spoke. "It was one of the challenges. I really didn't want to do it at first."

Chase recalled her face from inside the trailer. He'd

only caught a glimpse of her, but she'd looked crushed. He'd been terrified that somehow he'd caused that much pain in her life. It had tortured him over the last few hours.

Her arms tightened, and her chest rose in a sigh. He glanced down, unsure what it all meant.

"I'm so glad I did," she said more quietly, like she was sharing something deeply personal.

Chase cautiously lifted one hand and rested it gently on her head, loving the touch of her smooth curls. He'd always loved her, but it'd been nothing like what was pounding in his heart now, as if he would drop to his knees with the strength of it.

"That's incredible, Abigail," he whispered, hearing the husky sound of his voice. But there was no escape from the emotions that were coursing through him, and her contentment in his arms was utterly confusing. Did she want him back? Would she even consider it?

He felt frozen, unable to step away from the pure comfort of her embrace. But then, she wasn't pulling away either. With a shaking breath, he touched her face softly, tracing his fingertips along her smooth skin and tilting her chin upward.

She looked steadily into his eyes, still leaning against him with her arms around his back.

He paused when she released him, but instead of stepping away, her hands smoothed along each side of his face, and she pulled him down to meet her lips.

The shock of her soft kiss was an answer to all his questions but a portal to hundreds more. He shut off his brain and held her gently, kissing her like he never had before. It twisted his insides and scattered his thoughts delightfully, until she giggled and leaned away, leaving him wanting more.

Her eyes said as much too, and her cheeks were flushed with pink. It transformed her normal beauty into pure brilliance.

He grinned along with her, not sure what to say next. But one thing he knew. If she wanted this house by the ocean, she could have it. If she needed him to build it, he'd build it. He'd build her a hundred houses if it would make her happy. Because there wasn't anything in the world stronger than the truth he'd just uncovered, and he shared it with her along with another kiss.

"I love you, Bee," he whispered, overwhelmed by the sudden shine in her eyes and softness in her smile.

She held his face again, tangling her hands in his hair and pulling him close, resting her lips at his ear. "I love you too."

He couldn't tell if she was laughing or crying as he lifted her, letting her perfect feet dangle above the ground. It felt like a dream, and going back to work was the last thing on his mind.

When Mark yelled at him from the back porch, Chase ignored him.

"Sorry, uh—*friend of the owner*." Mark laughed. "We need one more hand for this install."

Chase set Abby back down, and she backed out of his arms, laughing again. "Go ahead," she said, squeezing his hand. "It's fine."

He leaned in, kissing her firmly and leaving with a grin on his lips. When he glanced back, she was watching him with a smile still lighting her face, and it made his head spin.

"Don't mean to break all that up," Mark teased, "but if it's any consolation, we're almost finished here."

Chase got to work, doing what he'd done a hundred times before but thinking of something completely new. A life with Abby. A ring he'd saved for her. And a future he'd almost given up on.

* * *

The evening had been one he wouldn't soon forget, perhaps forever. They'd spent hours talking and laughing, sometimes just getting lost in each other's eyes. It still didn't seem real, and Chase grumbled as he drove away that he should have stayed longer. Running home because he had an early morning client wasn't the most romantic move in the world.

He'd tried to pay attention to everything his long-time client said that morning, but in the end, he could hardly remember a word.

It seemed only a few minutes had passed instead of hours, and finally he was on his way back to Abby. All he could think of was her beautiful face and soft lips, and how his heart had burned the entire evening with the idea that she still wanted him. It felt like something completely new, or at least an entirely different level. Each kiss burned on his lips and sent his heart pounding. He couldn't wait to hold her in his arms again, where she fit perfectly.

When he pulled up to the house, something seemed strangely off. It was nearly ten o'clock with no sign of the work trucks. There were a couple of windows open as well, which wasn't easily explained seeing as how it'd been such a rainy night.

He stepped from his car and looked closer, noticing a strip of siding had been snapped off the side of the house —broken in two.

Had the wind picked up in the night?

Abby's trailer was bound to need a few repairs if so, but in one glance he could see the trailer was fine. He made his way around the back, finding the patio door wide open. When he caught sight of the inside of the house he flinched back, standing frozen in the doorway.

Rubble and broken bits of wood were scattered across the brown paper that covered the floor. Dark paint had been smeared across the walls, with the remnants of handprints making it clear they'd just slopped it on. The word *out* was visible more than once, making Chase swell with anger.

But it wasn't until he noticed a deep red streak that his heart started to pound. It didn't look like paint.

"Abigail?" he called, stepping across broken, splintered wood. A few of the carved rungs of the staircase had been broken in the middle and jutted out at awkward angles. Chase's breath was coming faster as he imagined a baseball bat or crowbar. "You here?"

He hoped she was still asleep, although he knew how much she loved getting up before the sun. One glance into the kitchen revealed more red streaks, leading to a large rabbit. It was left in the center of the room in the same condition of all the animals before it. But one thing was different now. Whoever was doing this had come inside the house, and by way of force… making it a whole new game.

Chase dug his phone from his jacket and typed a text quickly, sending it to Abigail. A phone chimed from upstairs and his eyes widened.

Why hadn't she answered him?

He dashed for the stairway, taking them three at a time. "Bee!" he shouted, fear pounding in his head. "Where are you?" The first bedroom was small and clearly empty. He rushed to the second, third, and fourth. As he made his way to the last three rooms, he finally heard a noise. A quiet sound like the scuffing of a shoe. He froze and listened, hardly able to hear over the beating of his heart and rush of his breath.

There it was again, a quiet sniff. He walked slowly into the last room down the hall. It's big, beautiful windows had been broken, leaving jagged sharp edges of glass clinging to their frames. Abby stood staring out at the broken view.

All his pent-up adrenaline left in a gust of breath, relief surging through him. "Abby," he breathed, pressing one hand to his chest as he tried to control his heart. "Are you okay? Are you hurt? Where is everyone?"

He took a small step forward with each question, still frantic to see her face and assure she was well. When he was directly beside her, he could see the tears that had fallen were now dried, leaving faint trails down her cheeks.

"I told them not to bother," she said. Her voice was bland, and she still stared out at the view. He touched her arm, and she took a quick breath, glancing down at the floor. "You were right, then," she said in the same dull, lifeless voice. "I never should have bought this house—it was a mistake."

THE SECRET OF POPPYRIDGE COVE

For the first time, Chase noticed a gold envelope in her hand with the top torn open.

"Why didn't I listen to you?" she continued, her eyes hesitantly meeting his.

Chase's heart throbbed at the sadness in her face, the depth seemed to completely overwhelm her. The joy and strength he'd admired only the day before were gone.

He held her arms, looking deeper into her endless brown eyes. "No, Abigail, I was wrong,"

She looked ready to object.

"I never should have put a limit on your dreams or told you what they should be. This place is different now, I can feel it. And maybe it always was, but now I see what you see. You can't quit."

She wasn't listening. Her face was still downturned and sinking deeper. She lifted the envelope in her hand. "I only read the first few lines, but it was enough."

He took the envelope, waiting for her to explain, but she merely looked out at the view again. There were two pages folded together, and quite a bit of writing. He glanced back at Abigail and opened them.

My dearest niece,

This, for you, is the last of your eight challenges. I only hope that my intended desire has come true and that your life will forever be the better for it. I know you must be eager to complete these challenges. Perhaps rushing through them. But there's something difficult that I must tell you. It may be hard to understand, but I want you to read this letter in its entirety before you curse my name.

There is no additional inheritance for you, my dearest Abigail. The initial sum was the entire amount. This will be hard to comprehend, but I do have my reasons for deceiving you. I hope you will accept my apology...

CHASE COULDN'T CONTINUE. He felt utterly betrayed but couldn't imagine what those words must have done to Abigail. She was still gazing at the view, almost trance-like. With a steadying breath, he reviewed her circumstances quickly. The amount of money still owed on the house was a sobering 1.5 million. The cost of expenses was on track until... he looked out at the broken windows.

Until today.

"Let's get out of here for a while," he suggested, feeling her despair almost tangibly.

She shrugged and allowed him to link his elbow with hers and walk her down the stairs. They stepped over the broken wood and glass, the noise echoing through the house eerily, but she didn't say a word.

Not until they'd reached her small trailer and made their way inside. When she sat down, Champ curled up at her feet, appearing to sense the trouble. "At least I have this," she said, gazing across the small space. "I should never have risked so much. It was foolish of me. Maybe I'm getting what I deserve."

Chase wasn't sure what to say. It was a dismal outlook, and he'd learned to recognize when it was time to stop. Like when he'd wanted that big house overlooking the Bay Bridge. It had been more luxurious than he'd ever imagined. But it would have meant working overtime for the rest of his life, and that was no life. Did he want her to be chained into a decision like this one?

With a breath, he worked on centering his thoughts. A reality where payments were made on a modest living and dreams were kept within a certain realm. His eyes drifted down to the counter where a stack of gold envelopes was set atop a long white one. He pulled out the white envelope slowly, glancing back at Abby. When he saw his name written on the front in her handwriting, he couldn't help but slide his finger under the seal.

CHAPTER 19

Abby woke suddenly, jolted from her dreams by the sound of car doors slamming. She blinked, hearing voices outside. They were loud and energetic, and before she had completely woken, there was a nail gun working and the sound of a tractor engine starting up.

She gazed across her small trailer, remembering Chase standing quietly in the kitchen, listening to her sulk. And then there was the truth about Aunt Sharalyn. It charged to the forefront of her mind like an assassin, eager to destroy any hope that may have been kindling within.

She groaned, wanting to pull the blanket over her head and sleep forever. It would be better than facing her life. But instead, she wandered to the small kitchen window to see three work trucks and a dumpster. Broken fragments of her house were being loaded up in a small tractor and discarded. In the back of one of the trucks were sheets of glass, strapped together and awaiting placement.

A mixture of confusion and irritation rushed over her. What were these people doing? Didn't they know she was out of money? She ran her hands through her hair and hurried out the door, wanting to stop everything before she was even more in debt.

Chase stood outside watching with Champ bounding in circles around him.

"Sit," he commanded, after glancing at Abby. The puppy plopped down beside him and held very still, except for his constantly twitching coat and tail. Like a ball of energy ready to explode. "Good. Stay." Chase pointed a finger at him and walked to meet Abby.

She glanced back at Champ. His ears were erect, but he didn't move. "Wow," she said, "that's some progress."

When she looked back into Chase's eyes, every memory of being in his arms and his kiss on her lips rushed back. Like a warm blanket, the memories wrapped her up in his love. She gazed back at him, suddenly speechless.

When a nail gun broke their trance, she gestured to the chaos behind them. "What's all this?" she asked. "They weren't even supposed to be here today—or ever again."

A grin broke across Chase's face, wide and dashing as if he'd been holding it back the whole time. It left Abby frozen in place. "You have enough to finish the repairs," he said easily. Simply, as if all the troubles she was experiencing were washed away with that one fact.

"Yes, but what about the money due? What about the first payment?" Abby was waiting for his smile to falter, but it didn't. "The mortgage is going to bury me, I know it. Especially since I quit my job to manage this place."

Still, Chase smiled. He lifted a white envelope with his name on the front and handed it to her. "I'm sorry, but I read your letter."

"Oh." Abby took the envelope, looking down at it and remembering her heartfelt words with a little embarrassment. "And this... changed something?"

"It changed everything," he answered quietly, taking her hand in his. "Dreams take effort. They take time. But they are one hundred percent worth fighting for."

She shook her head, feeling foolish for even trying something so drastic. What had she been thinking? "I'm sorry, Chase, but this is just way out of my ability. I wanted to design something incredible and have it take off in a matter of months, packed full of guests. But the reality is, I would need that inheritance just to keep things afloat for a while." She shrugged. "Without it, I'm too broke to even stand on the property here."

His smile was persistent. It gripped at the edges of her despair as if to pry it away. Her lip begrudgingly lifted on one side, and he leaned in closer, kissing her for a soft moment.

"I think we need to read the rest of Aunt Sharalyn's letter," he whispered, keeping his face so close, she could smell the slight pine fragrance on his skin.

She didn't want to read the letter. What else was there to say? Sharalyn lied. There was no more inheritance. End of story. Reluctantly, she agreed, walking back to the trailer with her arm around his back and his draped across her shoulder. It felt like wasted effort to read through an explanation from an eccentric aunt.

But she pulled out the papers anyway, unfolding them slowly and wishing it said something entirely new.

They didn't discuss it, and only sat together, laying the pages flat on the table in front of them. Abby read quickly, scanning across the words and the apology with a surge hesitant face. He fidgeted with his hands and finally glanced back at Abby, keeping his gaze on her as he spoke. "I was a little suspicious of her realtor, and it would explain why the animals were left here for so long prior. If perhaps he was hoping to snag the property in the future, but wasn't in quite the position to buy just yet?"

Abby shook her head. "Wait, Vance?" It sounded ridiculous. "He's the one who told me about the property in the first place, remember?"

"Yes," Chase agreed, "but that was when you were just a curious customer in a bread store. Most people don't have a couple million to spend on a house."

The policewoman had stayed quiet since they'd entered the kitchen, but now her eyes bored into Abby's. "So, I take it your realtor's name is Vance?"

Abby stiffened but nodded her head. "Yeah, he worked with me on the loan and even helped manage the remodel for the first couple weeks." Her cheeks were feeling warm, and she hoped it didn't show... and that the conversation would change topics soon.

The policewoman's eyebrows rose. "Ah, so he was hired to help you?" she asked, looking like she already knew the answer to her question was no.

Abby shook her head again. "He was helping as a friend only."

"Uh-huh," the officer tightened her lips. It was the closest thing to a smile Abby had seen on her yet. "And were you two romantically involved? Did he ever stay the night here on the property... with you?"

"What?" Abby gasped, "No! Of course not." She tried not to look at Chase, but her eyes flickered up to see the of contempt pressing her heart. What had Sharalyn been thinking? Why would this ever pass for a good idea? Now, instead of holding a job and working toward a future, she was broke and homeless.

She swallowed and turned the page over, continuing to read.

Chase sat next to her, scanning the pages quietly. But as Abby read, she started to hear the voice through the words. An aunt who had seen the turmoil of her niece's life and had gone to great lengths to craft a future for her. Each challenge had been specifically thought out and arranged as part of a bigger picture. A delicate balance of healing and hope that would allow something miraculous to happen.

Abby flipped to the last page.

I have lived a long life with many regrets. But one thing I know for certain was that fear prevented me from taking those big risks. Risks that I can see now, years later, would have been the very best part of my life. And instead, they are regrets. Things that could have been but never will be.

In putting you through these challenges, and giving you the absolute freedom to dream without limits, I wanted to create an environment where you would achieve the most possible with your capabilities—which are great—and live to enjoy the product of something most people never even try for.

Live this dream. Forge ahead without fear. And there will be no regrets.

All my love,
Aunt Sharalyn

. . .

hint of shock on his face. "I mean, he wanted to form a relationship, but I told him I wasn't interested."

"And that's it?" she pressed. "Why hasn't he continued helping with the remodel?"

"Well…" Abby felt completely embarrassed but knew she had to tell them everything. "He was pretty upset about it. I guess he thought I'd led him on, but I'd been trying to keep my distance. He was a little forceful about it, but then he left and I haven't seen him since."

"Uh-huh." The officer dipped her head, looking incredulous. "And you didn't find any of that suspicious at the time?"

Abby's embarrassment boiled over into anger, and she glared back. "No."

The policeman stepped forward. "So, when you say he helped with the remodel, what did he do exactly?" His voice was kind and calm, and Abby was finally able to think clearly.

"He just oversaw deconstruction and—" Abby paused, remembering something she suddenly realized would sound even more suspicious. "He put up the trail cam."

Eyes widened all around her, and she wondered if she'd been as naïve as their expressions said.

They returned to her trailer, and she played the small bit of video she had. But the officers didn't seem very interested in the footage of an arm. Instead, they asked her the same question a few times over.

"How could he be so terrible at placing a trail cam?" the policewoman asked again. "If you ask me, he purposely pointed it away from the yard."

"Was there anything else?" Chase spoke up for the first time since they'd left the house, and Abby watched his expression. It was hardened and serious, and he stared down the officers. "I assume you'll want to question the crew here, and the neighbors as well? That's a lot to get done. We'd better let you to it." He pulled the door open and stepped aside.

"Yes," the policeman finally replied. "We'll keep you informed of any developments. It might be best to stay the night in town tonight, just until we can get everything figured out.".

Abby let her breath out as the officers walked away, imagining Vance and what his reaction might be when he learned everything she'd told them. But when Chase closed the door, she could see him watching her out of the corner of her eye. She hesitated to look back at him, not until he'd walked slowly closer and stood directly in front of her. Then, she lifted her gaze to his face.

"Chase, nothing happened," she began, but he silenced her with a lifted hand and a shake of his head.

"You don't have to explain," he began. But he watched her face for a moment longer. "Just tell me one thing," he said.

"Okay." Abby's heart was beating, and she waited through a minute of silence that seemed to last forever, straining her brain to guess what he was going to ask.

"Define... *forceful*... for me," he said quietly, his gaze deep and unmoving.

"Oh." She was quickly thrown back into the memory of Vance's arms around her, locking her to him and refusing to budge when she tried to shake him off. "It could've been worse if you hadn't gotten here so quick that morning I called."

Chase's head tilted and his eyes narrowed, and Abby

was sure he was recalling Vance's manners and expression when he'd sped away from the property that morning.

"He just wasn't taking no for an answer. Not until you showed up." Her voice quieted to a whisper, and she rested her hands on his sides. "So, thank you."

She didn't have to pull him closer, he kissed her easily. "You should have told me," he whispered, touching her face softly. "He'd better not come around again."

Abby frowned. "I don't think he will." She hesitated, battling with her intuition. "Chase, I don't think he's the one behind this." She looked out the window and noticed one of the upstairs glass panels had already been replaced.

"Hmm…" Chase looked like he was considering her words, while at the same time not changing his opinion of Vance in the least. "Let's hope those police officers stumble across the person responsible. It's a completely different game now that they're breaking and entering."

"I know." Abby felt like lead had settled in her stomach, and as much as she tried to think it away, it remained.

"Should we run to *Le Coin* and pick up some decor? I know it's your favorite interior design shop in the state." He winked with a smile that invited back the energy Abby had been swimming in an hour earlier. Up until those officers stopped by.

"Sure." Abby smiled. "Let's do it."

CHAPTER 20

The afternoon was waning when they loaded Abby's car up with decor that she felt easily defined her soul. Everything was neutral modern, with a slight industrial flair, and above all it was rustic. The perfect marriage of past and future. It would fit the property beautifully.

"Should we meet back in a couple of hours?" Chase offered. "I've only got one patient, so it won't take long. Might need to schedule a couple meetings."

"Okay." Abby squeezed into the driver's seat. It had been moved forward to fit the pileup of everything from metal vases to throw pillows. "I'll see you in a few!" She waved at Chase, loving the way his cheeks turned a slight pink in the crisp autumn air.

All the way back, she thought of him. The way he spoke to her, looked at her, held her... even the threat he'd breathed against Vance was incredible. Because it was for her.

When she arrived back at the house, the sky was just

beginning to dim, and lights were being set up around the property. Abby wondered what Chase had said to them. Obviously, it was something amazing to have them working around the clock the way they were.

She began loading bags into her trailer, one after the other. It almost filled up the small space. On the last trip, she glanced into the dark trees and stopped in her tracks.

Champ wasn't on his chain. She hurried and tossed the last bag inside before whistling for him and waiting with one ear turned to the wind.

Nothing.

"Champ!" she shouted, clapping her hands until they echoed through the trees. She held perfectly still, listening. But there was no sound besides the occasional hoot of an owl. Her heart liked to overreact, and it raced away, giving her permission to imagine every horrible thing that could have happened.

She walked forward until she passed the first row of trees and was covered by a blanket of quiet. Even the workers behind her seemed to be whispering. "Champ?" she called.

Suddenly, out of the silence, a noise echoed through the trees. Quick and sharp, and then it was gone. Like a pained yelp.

She listened more intently, waiting for another signal of where he might be, or if it was even him. "Champ!" She had tried to yell, but her voice came out in a raspy whisper. Another yelp followed, more clear this time.

It was Champ. And he'd heard her.

She dashed into the trees, running as softly as she could in case he made another noise. The forest floor was damp and cold, quieting her steps. The pepper spray back in her cabin came to her mind, but she heard a high-pitched whine and kept running. Whatever was hurting him, she'd find it.

* * *

CHASE FELT BAD ABOUT LYING, but he knew he couldn't tell Abigail where he was headed. He stood outside Vance's office and tried to control his anger. It surged through him, threatening to scatter his thoughts and blur his decisions. He took another breath, attempting to clear his head.

"Right this way, sir." A cheerful secretary led him to an open office door, and he stepped inside to see Vance seated at his desk, looking down at his computer screen. He imagined Vance's hands on Abigail and his own hands clenched into fists.

Vance finally looked up. He rolled his chair back in surprise, and after a moment, he gestured to the chair across from him. "Please, have a seat."

Chase sat, keeping his eyes glued to Vance for any signs of guilt. He couldn't help but think his realtor job and abundant knowledge of the house pointed a pretty accusing finger at him. And then to hear he'd been the one to place the trail cam. It was completely condemning in Chase's mind.

"What can I do for you?" Vance asked.

Chase thought he could see a tremor in the calm lines of Vance's face, but overall, he seemed incredibly good at smoothing over any visible emotion... which made Chase suspect him even more.

He cleared his throat. "I'm going to be very direct

here," he warned, working to keep the anger in his chest from spreading to his voice. "Someone broke into the Poppyridge house last night, leaving it vandalized. There was also a dead rabbit deposited in the kitchen and warnings written on the walls."

But the guilt Chase hoped to glimpse never came, and instead, Vance gripped the desk with both hands.

"What?" His mouth was slack and utterly shocked. "Is Ms. Tanner okay?"

Chase wanted to punch him in his bewildered face, but he swallowed back the irrational thought. "She's fine," he shifted in his seat, suddenly eager to get back to Abigail. He hadn't meant to take so long, and judging by what he perceived as fake innocence radiating from Vance, it was going to take a while.

He squared his shoulders and leaned forward, glaring. "Did you have anything to do with it?" he asked, not caring if it sounded like a threat. He had to know.

One of Vance's eyebrows rose dramatically, but gradually he appeared to recover. "You're seriously asking me this?" He looked back long enough to see Chase nod. "Me? The one who showed her the house. The one who negotiated the sale. You think I'm now trying to drive her away?" He laughed suddenly in a quick, angry burst. "And why would I do that? I've been protecting her this whole time—she doesn't even know the half of it." He stood from his chair and turned to the window, crossing his arms in front of him. "I don't owe you an explanation. This isn't an interrogation."

Chase stood as well. "No, it isn't. Would you like it to be?"

This time when Vance turned, there was a break in his

calmness. His eyes flickered to Chase's arms, and the way his T-shirt strained when he crossed them in front of his chest.

"Look," he said angrily, "I've admired the house for a long time, but it's not in my means to buy the thing. You come across stuff like this every day in my line of work. There's a dream home around every corner, you just learn to go about your day."

"Hmm..." Chase's eyes narrowed as he studied the expression on Vance's face. "So, what have you been protecting her from, then?"

Vance threw his hands in the air. "From theories. History. Stuff you come across when you dig in and research a property. And since this one was a gold mine sitting on the market for years on end, I did my homework." He cast a wary eye at Chase and sat down again. "Turns out the place used to be haunted."

Chase's breath escaped in a *hmph*. "Right," he said, feeling like he'd wasted his time.

"I'm not saying it was, but people seemed to believe it. Here—" He opened a desk drawer and pulled a thick file from it. "See for yourself. Go ahead... and show Abbs. It's all there. It explains why it never sold."

"So, why didn't you tell her this?" Chase asked, opening the file and glancing down at a newspaper article.

Vance shrugged. "I didn't want it clouding her judgment. She fell completely in love with the place. And ghost stories are kind of a downer."

Chase tucked the file under his arm and nodded back at Vance. "Thanks," he mumbled, heading back through the building and to his car.

After he'd closed the doors and started the engine, he opened the folder again. There was a bundle of papers, and he flipped through them quickly. Most were police transcriptions of buyer's testimonies about the property, which he didn't find particularly helpful. Some of them sounded anxious to cause a stir, like they were only after attention. He rifled back to the first page, a newspaper article. It was nearly forty years old, stained and faded. A large picture was set into the story, and Chase scanned over the words quickly.

It was an account from a local resident, and Vance had been right. The man was very convinced. He spoke of vicious beings and how to ensure they didn't cross from the *mansion* to any neighboring homes.

It was crazy.

The way the man spoke had chills breaking out on Chase's arms. He sounded nearly insane. Going on and on about evil spirits and why they preferred abandoned houses over occupied ones. He explained what would happen if the house were to sell, and Chase felt a dull shock radiating through him. Breathing harder, he took a moment to really look at the image.

The man was in classic 90s fashion, short-sleeve, plaid button-up shirt and jeans. His hands were on his hips, and Chase scanned over his arms before catching a glimpse of something. A dark spot on the page. He moved the image closer to the window until it was illuminated by sunlight.

And there, above his wrist on the inside of his forearm... was a tattoo of three stars, staggered together. Chase's head spun, and he read over the caption for the first time.

Harold Fillmore, Neighbor of the Poppyridge Mansion.

His mouth went dry, and his breath was suddenly hard to control. He pressed Abigail's number on his phone, listening to it ring while he pulled away from the curb with a screech.

* * *

Abby was getting close. She could hear a scratching sound not far off, but she circled around, staying behind shrubs and trees. Still, it was hard to see anything in the encroaching darkness. Her heart pounded, but she refused to turn back and leave Champ out in the woods alone.

Finally, she caught a glimpse of something. A quick movement in the brush. It was directly above a fallen log, nestled between two trees. She inched her way forward, constantly searching the darkness while honing in on whatever was causing the movement. When she was a few steps away, she recognized Champ's tail whipping back and forth.

She abandoned all caution and rushed forward, relief and fear flowing through her simultaneously, and dropped to the log to see him stretched out on the ground. His head was lifted and staring directly at her as if he'd heard her coming, and his tail whipped back and forth excitedly. But his front leg was caught in a rope, tied so tight it had started to sink through and bleed on one side. He'd stretched his body as far away from the offending rope as he could and lay on the ground, still pulling at his leg.

Abby dropped down, rubbing his head. "Hey, boy," she whispered, "Let's get outta here." She glanced up, frightened when she could barely see past the few trees around her. Darkness was falling fast.

The rope was fastened to a cord, which had tightened severely around his leg. She had to look a second time before she realized what she was up against. "It's a snare," she whispered, trying to coax Champ closer to loosen the tension. He whined and backed away again, cinching it tight on his leg. "Hold on," she pleaded, pulling and dragging him close enough to create some slack in the rope.

She found a thin stick and wedged it under the crossing-point of the cord around his leg. With a small back and forth movement, she was able to move it up in small segments. She held firm to Champ's leg at the same time, assuring he couldn't pull the trap tight again. Finally, it looked large enough, and she carefully maneuvered Champ's leg in one hand and the snare in the other, hoping to slip his paw through without catching it up on the rope.

"Hey!" A voice shouted from directly behind the trees, followed by the rushing sound of footsteps. Abby screamed, dropping everything.

Champ reacted fast, darting out from the snare before it could tighten again. Abby dove over the log, just catching sight of someone behind her. A hand gripped her shoe, and she kicked it off, scrambling to her feet.

"That's my kill!" The voice screeched again, deep and frantic.

Abby glanced behind her as she ran, seeing a dark outline of a man hurling over the log and toward her. Frantic, she followed Champ's shadowy outline. But he was racing away, with eyes much more adapted to the dark. And he was quickly fading.

A branch whipped across Abby's face, and she ducked down, placing a hand over the pain. The footsteps had stopped behind her, but she ran as fast as she could manage in the dark, finally catching a glimpse of the construction lights.

Suddenly the man barreled through the trees beside her, slamming her down.

"Champ!" she screamed, bringing her knees up and using all her force to hurl him off of her. He grabbed at her arms, pushing her back into a tree trunk.

"You threaten everything!" he shouted, leaning in close enough that she could just make out his features.

"Mr... Fillmore?" Her knees were shaking and his hands squeezed her arms so tightly, crushing her. "Let go," she pleaded. "I'm your neighbor. Abigail."

"No!" His eyes were wild, and he shook her with each word. "You will have them attacking our homes. That dog is the only creature that will keep them satisfied, and you've ruined it!"

Abby was gasping with the tree's bark grinding into her back. Whatever was going on with Mr. Fillmore, he clearly wasn't himself.

He leaned in, inches from her face.

"Call your dog," he whispered, digging his fingers into her arms.

"You're hurting me," she said quietly, keeping her voice from shaking.

"Call him," he repeated, "or I'll take you instead."

Abby glanced down to see a large knife strapped to his waist. "Okay," she breathed. "Okay, I will," She looked into his face, fear radiating through her at the absolute rage in his eyes. "Just let me go so I can whistle for him." She kept her face calm, watching as he looked her over and finally stepped away.

She dropped down, digging with her hands and feet to scramble to the side. Pushing up, she turned to see him pull the knife from his belt. Screaming for help, she dove to the side, feeling something hit her shoulder. But she didn't stop, barreling through the branches and brush until coming out again on open ground and running with all her strength.

Mr. Fillmore was shouting. She could hear him getting closer, and she glanced at the construction lights longingly. They were far to the left, but she couldn't risk turning around. She could hear him behind her, so close it was terrifying. How was he able to keep up with her at his age?

She felt so weak and tired. Her muscles ached, and her head swam. It wasn't until she stumbled to a stop that she realized she was bleeding. Her shirt was seeped in it. Wet, warm, sticky blood. She swayed on her feet, and the footsteps behind her paused.

"I'm sorry to do this," she heard him say, breathing heavily. "I wanted the dog, but now I have no choice."

She could sense him close behind her, his footsteps falling like the ticking of a clock. Her final countdown until he was directly behind her. Her head swam, and she closed her eyes at his intake of breath. But the pain never came, and in her hazy mind, there was shouting. So many voices. And lights. They flashed in her eyes, and she held her hands up, shading the brightness. She recognized the policewoman who had scowled. Construction workers shouted back and forth. Too much shouting.

She swayed again, and someone held her arms. It was a

relief to let them help. She sagged into their grip and eagerly borrowed their strength.

"Abigail." His voice was whispered, close to her face and full of a compassion that woke her senses. She could feel his arms around her, familiar now, and she held on to him. "Stay awake," Chase urged, "listen to my voice. Just a few steps. That's it."

Settled into a chair, Abby felt a sharp pain starting to break through her foggy mind. Chase still had his arm linked with hers, and she smiled, finally meeting his eyes. "It was Fillmore," she said. Her voice was dry and scratchy. He signaled to one of the policemen and handed her a bottled water. She took a quick sip of the cool, healthy liquid.

"I know," he finally answered. "They've taken him back to the police station after talking to his daughter. Apparently, he's been having trouble staying on his medication since his wife died a couple of years ago."

A paramedic knelt in front of them along with the familiar policewoman. The young man began cutting her sweatshirt sleeve open.

"Do you want to press charges ma'am?" the policewoman asked. She stood, looking authoritative and strong, hands on her hips.

"I…" Abby paused. "I don't know."

"Uh-huh," the officer said. She sounded less than excited about it, but she did show the beginnings of a smile when Abby looked up at her. "Well, here's what I know. This Mr. Fillmore—your neighbor. You've met, correct?"

Abby nodded, glancing down at her arm as the paramedic gave her a quick shot. She'd never really minded finished off the last stitch and placed a bandage across her shoulder.

"There you go, ma'am." He smiled and collected his things.

"We can take my car back if you'd like," the policewoman offered. She linked her arm with Abby's, helping her up carefully with Chase on the other side.

Abby thought suddenly of her mom. Perhaps if she'd gotten help… if there had been a medication for her suffering, she could have been a good mom. Lived a good life.

They walked slowly toward the patrol car with the beam of a flashlight to guide them.

"I don't want to press charges," Abby said quietly. It felt right the moment she'd said the words, and she glanced at Chase to see him smiling back at her. He squeezed her gently.

"Hmm." The policewoman lapsed back into silence, but when a light from her squad car flashed across her face, Abby thought she saw a genuine smile.

needles, and the instant warmth and numbness were welcome.

"Right," the policewoman continued. "Well, he had an episode years and years ago. It was about the time your pretty little house was the subject of town gossip. And one day, Mr. Fillmore comes home frantic and out of sorts, convinced that the house on Poppyridge Cove was haunted, and he needed to burn it to the ground. You can imagine how Mrs. Fillmore felt about that."

Her smooth eyebrows arched in an exaggerated expression, giving her normally strict, bossy appearance a dash of beauty. "He was hospitalized for a couple of days, given some medication for the hallucinations, and has been on it ever since. His daughter did say he'd stopped taking it at one time and was thrown back into the very same person he'd been that day so many years prior. But his wife had always kept track of his pills. He insisted after her death that he was taking them and was fine, but it was all a lie."

It was a lot to think about. Abby's mind went around in circles, imagining everything from Mr. Fillmore's perspective, repeating what he'd said to her and how he'd acted all these years. Depositing animals to appease the haunted house.

"Didn't people realize it was him?" Abby asked, wondering how that little detail could have escaped all the police officers she'd called to her house.

"Well, no, it's been so many years. I wouldn't even have the information if his daughter hadn't confided in me. Had to dig pretty deep to find any documentation on it."

"I see." Abby's thoughts were slowing, analyzing everything now that she was free from the pain. The paramedic

CHAPTER 21

Six months later

ABBY STOOD JUST inside the front door, holding it open while a father carried three suitcases and trailed after his wife and four kids. The children giggled and chattered, their voices echoing through the open space pleasantly.

A large fire crackled at the far end of the room, proof that the spring had been unseasonably cool. But the persistent fog had lifted in time to leave sunlight pouring in through the lineup of massive windows above.

"Thank you," the man said, smiling at her and nodding his head in appreciation. Their happy group bumbled up the stairs together, a non-stop chorus of giggles.

"They're a happy group," Chase said.

Abby spun around to see him walking from the kitchen with his green 'kiss the cook' apron dusted in flour. She heeded the message and wrapped her arms around his neck, kissing him long enough to have her thoughts fading. But not completely. There was an especially persistent one she couldn't let go of.

"So, are you going to tell me what you're up to yet?" She leaned to the side, trying to catch a glimpse into the kitchen.

"No, you don't." He grinned and kissed her forehead. "C'mon, I need a quick break, anyway. But I have to be back in twenty minutes." He pulled the timer from his apron pocket, proof of the countdown.

A tight grin stretched across her lips as she tried to give him a stern look through her happiness. It never worked.

On the back porch were two white swinging benches and a few rocking chairs. The brilliant white contrasted beautifully against the gray-blue of the siding, and paired with the ocean air, it was magnificent.

Champ's head lifted from where he'd been curled up on the sunny end of the deck, and he padded over to meet them, circling them four times in his excitement before finally stopping to accept affection. "Hey, boy." Abby paused to rub his favorite spot on the side of his neck. "Let's go!"

He leaped down the stairs and pranced in place, visibly frustrated at their slow pace. The walk was familiar, a cobbled pathway through their grass that met with a sandy trail. Posts on either side were worn and perfectly imperfect, strung with rope and occasionally tilted. They stopped only to slip their shoes off—a feat that they could easily accomplish while holding hands.

Their cove was vacant even though the sun had shown itself clearly now, beaming hot and strong on their skin.

* * *

CHASE LOVED the feel of her hand in his, smooth and delicate. He glanced down at her, imagining a day when she would be dressed in white, looking back at him. Her eyes were on the ocean—they always were. She seemed constantly mesmerized by it as if searching for a treasure in the crest of a distant wave.

"Are you sure you want an outdoor ceremony?" he asked, transfixed on her quick smile.

"I do," she answered calmly.

He tightened his arm around her, holding her close against him. "You don't think our guests will freeze to death or be blown away in a gust of wind?"

Her body shook gently as she laughed. "No, that won't happen." She tilted her head and looked up at him. "I trust the universe to give us a peaceful, beautiful beginning."

Champ dug his paws through the sand and sat down next to them, looking out at the water as well. He was a very good-natured dog, and the thought made Chase smile. "Well, if there's one thing I've learned about you, Bee, it's to trust your instincts." He sighed. "An outdoor wedding, it is."

She leaned back against his chest. "Can you believe it? I hardly can, so much has happened in a few short months."

His fingertip slid across the ring on her hand, "Yes, it has, and none of it was what I'd expected. More like a wishful dream that managed to come true." He tucked his head aside hers, giving her a full hug and swaying to some imaginary melody. "I wish I could have been the one to give you everything you wanted, especially this house. Surprising that the very person trying to keep you away would end up leaving you enough money to finish the remodel and then some."

"Mr. Fillmore didn't know what he was doing before, how could I blame him for that? He'd been off his medication for nearly two years, and no one knew. His mind wasn't right. I can understand that."

ABBY THOUGHT back to her childhood, wondering if she was just imagining it or if the pain had dulled even more. Perhaps this tiny bit of grace she'd extended to Mr. Fillmore would be a healing ointment to her past.

She glanced back at Chase. "He's got a kind heart," she finished, coming quickly back to the present.

"How's he doing?" Chase asked, pausing when a beeping rhythm vibrated in his pocket. He silenced it quickly, and they started a lazy walk back. "Do you want to visit him tonight?"

Abby reached for his hand. "I was planning on it. He's enjoying the facility, it's very comfortable. And he's closer to his daughter but still independent, which they both like. It's an ideal situation."

"And thanks to your kindness, he's able to live out the rest of his life in peace."

Abby shrugged. "It wouldn't feel right to see him go to jail."

Chase nodded. "Very true, but also very genuine of

you." He stepped up his pace and pulled her with him. "We need to hurry if you want your birthday cake to be absolute perfection."

"Okay, but—" She swayed back, forcing him to stop, although he glanced anxiously at the house. "Just one more thing. I want you to know this." She lifted her eyebrows pointedly and waited until she had his full attention. "You *have* given me everything I've ever wanted, Chase. *Everything*. Just knowing your heart and having you with me… that's all I need. The house is just wood and nails." She grinned. "A genius told me that once."

"Oh yeah? A genius, huh?" He stepped in next to her, and his eyes stilled. A smile pulled at his mouth, and gently touching her face, he lowered his lips to hers. "Well, can I share this wood and nails house with you?"

"Absolutely." She felt so drawn to his warmth, it was impossible to resist leaning in, and her eyes brushed closed just as their lips met.

His kisses were different now, with some mystical ingredient that hadn't been there before. Somehow their time apart had awoken something inside her. A realization of her connection to him, and of how much deeper it ran. Deep enough to have her feeling torched inside, burning her lungs and throat with a delicious heat.

Her hands settled gently against his sides, and like an afterthought, she was distracted by his strength. The defined ridges of muscle he seemed to think nothing of. But just as her hands slid to his back, he stepped away.

"We have to keep walking," he whispered, slightly out of breath. He took a step back toward the house, pulling her with him and kissing her again, taking another step.

She stumbled over her feet, laughing as she walked. "Okay, but really I don't mind overbaked."

"Ah, never." He shook his head, "It will be perfection. Just like this." He stopped, standing in place, and held her face gently in his hands. His eyes were soft, looking over her with an expression that was honest and easy to read. It told her a hundred different things, although they were all the same.

He loved her.

Above everything else, she knew this completely. Her hands settled over his, and she was lost in one final kiss. It sunk deep into her heart, dangerously close to her soul. The kind of kiss that had her letting go of everything she held so tightly, the things that kept her safe from the world. They drifted away without a thought.

When they walked back into the house, it was filled with a sweet, rich fragrance. Chase gave her a look that barely contained the excitement bubbling inside him and rushed off to the kitchen, forbidding her to follow.

Half the fun was allowing him to surprise her, and she planned on letting him.

Giggles and sounds of movement came from upstairs, and the fireplace held only a crumble of embers glowing with deep orange heat. Abby sat on the hearth, feeling it warm her back as the sunset mimicked its color from outside. She fingered the delicate stone on her left hand. A warmth flowed through her, coming from some internal source. It left her with fleeting thoughts of Chase, and every glance he'd ever given her. The love that had been there all along.

And finally, she was home.

. . .

*Did you love your experience with The Secret of Poppyridge Cove? Please consider leaving a review. Every single bit of praise keeps me going. Thank you, thank you.

*Jump into book two now A Traitor at Poppyridge Cove

Printed in Great Britain
by Amazon